Black Magic

An Arabian Stallion

Elizabeth Stitchway
Private Investigator Series
Book 2

MARY JANE FORBES

Todd Book Publications

Mary Jane Forbes

The Arabian Horse

The Arabian is a breed of horse that originated on the Arabian Peninsula. With a distinctive head shape and high tail carriage, the Arabian is one of the most easily recognizable horse breeds in the world.

Arabian horses have refined, wedge-shaped heads, a broad forehead, large eyes, large nostrils, and small muzzles. Most display a distinctive concave or "dished" profile. Many Arabians also have a slight forehead bulge between their eyes, called the "jibbah" by the Bedouin, that adds additional sinus capacity, believed to have helped the Arabian horse in its native dry desert climate. Another breed characteristic is an arched neck with a large, well-set windpipe set on a refined, clean throatlatch. This structure of the poll and throatlatch was called the *mitbah* or *mitbeh* by the Bedouin, and in the best Arabians is long, allowing flexibility in the bridle and room for the windpipe.

Other distinctive features are a relatively long, level croup, or top of the hindquarters, and naturally high tail carriage. Well-bred Arabians have a deep, well-angled hip and well laid-back shoulder. Most have a compact body with a short back. Some, though not all, have 5 lumbar vertebrae instead of the usual 6, and 17 rather than 18 pairs of ribs. Thus, even a small Arabian can carry a heavy rider with ease. Arabians usually have dense, strong bone, sound feet, and good hoof walls. They are especially noted for endurance, and the superiority of the breed in Endurance riding competition demonstrates that well-bred Arabians are strong, sound horses with good bone and superior stamina. At international levels of FEI (International Federation for Equestrian Sports) sponsored endurance events, Arabians and half-Arabians are the dominant performers in distance competition worldwide.

Wikipedia

Prologue

MOONLIGHT PENETRATED THE glass curtain covering the bedroom window. Jerry and Barbara Stevens tossed fitfully until after midnight, finally falling into a deep sleep. The night sky was filled with stars. The air was still. The temperature had dropped below forty degrees—normal for the beginning of January in Ocala, Florida.

Their eyes shot open—startled by the ring of the telephone.

"Jerry, it's time. Hurry, hurry." Barbara, already out of bed, pulled on her jeans, but Jerry was ahead of her—he had slept in his jeans. Struggling with a dark-green sweater, his head finally popped through. He slipped his bare feet into well-worn sneakers and shot out the door.

"Call Linda," he yelled over his shoulder.

"Her phone's programmed to ring at the same time as ours," she yelled back, her brown curls bouncing around her face as she ran. "I'm right behind you."

The two raced across the lawn to the barn. Jerry unlatched the barn door sliding it open along its rails. Flicking on the light switch, he stepped inside onto scattered pieces of hay strewn on the cement floor. Barbara, now beside her husband, quickly walked with him to the door of the large center stall.

The mare, lying on a fresh covering of hay, gave a soft whinny as Jerry and Barbara approached her.

"It's okay, Princess, we're here. Good girl." Barbara kept her voice low as she knelt down by the pregnant mare's head stroking her golden neck. Jerry slowly circled to the far side of the stall. "Anything happening yet?" Barbara whispered.

"No. Wait. Yes, yes. I can just see it."

Princess raised her head from the sweet-smelling hay looking back across her body.

Barbara heard Linda's truck pull to stop, the door open and close, and then Linda entered the barn. Luckily the veterinarian's equine center was only a few miles from the Stevens' farm. Golden Princess had been under her care since the minute she had inseminated the mare eleven months earlier with semen collected from a champion Arabian stallion.

"Hello, Princess. How're you doing?" Linda said softly, as she circled the stall trading places with Jerry.

"I think everything looks good so far," Jerry said, moving away a few steps to give Linda a better vantage point in case the mare needed her help, otherwise she would not intervene.

The three humans talked quietly as Princess continued to look back, waiting to see her foal—the contractions continued. The night was hushed in anticipation, even the katydids stopped their music—all quietly waiting for Mother Nature to take her course.

"Here we come," Linda said, crouching down in her brown leather boots. Her long blonde hair was tied back in a ponytail, a few wisps sticking out that she missed in her haste to leave her house.

"There ... a hoof broke through the sac ... here comes the other ... and look at that baby's muzzle will you." Linda gently pulled the broken sac back a notch. The whole head eased forward, bobbed up and down, staring into the dim light of his new home. He gasped a couple of times, his lungs filling with air.

"He's breathing nicely. When he starts through the birth canal his chest is compressed. With the first gulps of breath the lungs inflate," Linda explained. "One more contraction and he should be free of his mother ... there."

The foal inched forward on the hay bumping against his mother. He stopped to rest, then inched forward again onto the mare's leg—Princess nickered softly encouraging her baby but she still couldn't reach him. He kept moving forward, always pausing to rest. Finally Princess could nuzzle the baby. She began to lick the fetal membranes from his face, then carefully cleaned away the rest of the sac from his body.

Linda sat on the hay next to the baby, quickly testing the foal's heart and respiratory rate, all the time cooing to Princess what a good girl she was. "Oh, he's a strong one," she whispered smiling up at Jerry. "Let's give the mother and baby a little time to bond. Everything is textbook so far."

Barbara took Jerry's hand. They smiled at each other, both letting out a quiet sigh of relief that the foal was healthy. They weren't thinking of the several thousands of dollars they had invested in the purchase of the frozen semen, or the delicate insemination procedure that Linda had performed. They were caught up in the wonder of seeing this foal in his first few minutes of life. He showed spunk, vitality, and beautiful coloring—all velvety black. Of course it would be a few months before they would know if his breeding from two champions had produced a winner worthy of showing in a ring. At this moment that didn't matter because they had immediately fallen in love with the little guy.

"Princess seems to be taking our presence in stride," Linda said. "Sometimes a new mother will get a bit fidgety with people around her baby. I'm finished with the first tests," she said putting her instruments back in her worn, brown-leather bag. "Let's stand back and let Princess and her baby get to know each other."

Barbara glanced at her watch. "I can't believe it's only been forty minutes since the phone woke us up."

"The birth goes fast once the water breaks," Linda said. "Typically around twenty minutes."

Jerry gazed at the newest member of his farm. "We about jumped out of our skins when our phone rang, triggered by that device you implanted into Princess to alert us when her water broke."

"I was a bit startled myself when my cell started playing my ringtone," Linda said laughing. "You'd think I would be used to it by now. Andy and I rarely get a full night's sleep."

The foal inched up on his sternum, not quite ready to try his legs. Princess nuzzled him and he responded with a soft whinny. Hearing this, Princess carefully got to her feet, and as she did the umbilical cord broke away a few inches from the foal's body. Linda was ready and dipped the end of the stump into a disinfectant to ward off infection.

"I'll leave some of this with you, Jerry. I want you to apply it a few times today. I'll stop by again later this afternoon to be sure he's still doing well and check the stump end again."

"Linda, do you have time for a quick cup of coffee?" Barbara asked.

"I'd love one, thank you."

"I'll scoot into the tack room and brew a quick pot for us. Be back in a minute," Barbara backed out of the stall not wanting to take her eyes from the fuzzy colt. A few minutes later she returned with three mugs of steaming hot coffee. "Look, look, he's trying to stand up. Whoa, a little unsteady there," she laughed handing the mugs to the vet and Jerry.

"I think you're going to have a prancing, frisky Arabian on your hands," Linda said, taking a sip of coffee. "He's showing off already, happy to be out of the womb."

"Jerry, look, he's trying to find the udder."

"He's not exactly going to the right end," Jerry said chuckling.

"Ah, but watch Princess, she's guiding him with her hind leg. There he goes. Not bad for his first attempt—a little milk on his nose," Linda said, draining the remains of coffee from her cup. "Well, guys, I think I'll be on my way. As you know he'll probably bounce around for twenty minutes at a time, then lie down and rest between the little romps for a day or two. As I said, I'll pop over at the end of the day, but from the looks of everything so far, I think you have yourselves a healthy foal. Watch him closely for the next few hours to see that he's actually swallowing some of her milk."

Jerry and Barbara walked the vet out to her car. "Thanks, Linda, for driving over so quickly. I think I speak for Barbara and I that we already love the little fella and from the looks of him he could mean big things as a show horse."

"I believe you're right. See you later."

They watched the truck's receding taillights as Linda headed down the driveway. "Jerry, it's a beautiful night—only four o'clock. The sun won't be up for several hours."

"I'm going back in the barn, sit awhile at the end of the stall to make sure Princess and the foal get along okay," Jerry said wrapping his arms around his wife in a bear hug.

Barbara leaned away and looked into her husband's eyes. "Hey, don't think I'm not coming with you. I don't want to miss a minute of these first hours of his life."

Chapter 1

———

Two-and-a-half Years Later

AUGUST USHERED IN the first heat-wave of summer. Hot, humid air enveloped the Turner Equine Reproduction Center. The temperature stood at a stifling seventy-nine degrees at 3:28 a.m.

Linda bolted upright in bed. "Andy, wake up." She shook her husband's shoulder straining to hear the noise again.

"What's the matter, honey?" Andy rolled over putting his arm around his wife's waist pulling her stiff body toward him.

"One of the horses whinnied. I think it was Trumpet." Linda threw the sheet off and on bare feet ran to the open bedroom window.

The half moon shone brightly through a layer of thin clouds casting shadows over the pastures of the equine center. A slight breeze orchestrated a flutter dance of the live oak leaves brushing through Linda's white cotton nightshirt. She stood in the shadows behind the gauzy curtain as it moved ever so slightly in the humid air.

Andy sat up in bed, yawning deeply. "It's only 3:30. Maybe Trumpet was spooked by a raccoon. They like to wander around in the middle of the night."

"I don't see anything and he seems content grazing on the hay. Maybe you're right." She padded back to bed lying down beside her husband. He cradled her in his arms and was instantly breathing heavily, sound asleep. Linda's eyes remained open, but soon her lids grew heavy, and she fell into a restless sleep.

———

MONDAYS WERE ALWAYS busy at the Turner Equine Reproduction Center. Leslie, the office manager, was already fielding calls—owners wanting to know if the insemination of their mare had resulted in an embryo. A man from Brazil called about the center's fees. He was interested in sending frozen semen from his award-winning Arabian stallion to breed with a Florida Arabian mare.

The air conditioner steadily pumped cool air into the office area of the building, but it was still uncomfortable. This August was proving to be one of the hottest and most humid on record boosting the heat index into triple digits. Leslie took the hand towel she kept tucked in the waistband of her jeans on days like this and wiped her forehead. It was just about time for their college intern to arrive for work, so Leslie hit the button routing calls to voicemail while she opened the doors for business.

Wiping her forehead again, Leslie walked to the door leading from the reception area to the examination room. She inserted the key, but the lock was already released. She wondered if Linda was in the laboratory which was attached to the examination room. She pushed the door open to say hello and to check the whiteboard with the day's list of horses to be seen. They had a full schedule—a pregnant mare due for an examination in the first stall. A mare in another stall was slated to begin the regimen of testing every six hours to catch her when she started to ovulate.

Leslie stepped through the door. Screamed. Her hands flew to her face. The intern was curled up on the cement floor. She ran to him. Knelt down beside him, shook his arm. His eyes were open— staring into space. "No, no, Rick." She fumbled for her cell phone, but she kept missing her pocket. Finally grabbing the phone, she punched Linda's code.

"Hi, Leslie, I was—"

"Linda, hurry. It's Rick ... I think he's dead."

———

LINDA AND ANDY RACED across the grassy divide between their house and the center's main building. Reaching the barn, which was attached to the back end of the office building, Andy inserted his key into the padlock and shoved the heavy barn door along its rails opening the stall area. They ran up the center of the barn, stalls on either side holding the patients scheduled for the day's examinations and treatments. Linda reached the door into the examination room jerking it open. Andy entered on her heels.

Linda rushing to Rick's side, tried to turn him onto his back, but he remained coiled. She felt the artery in his neck for a pulse. Without looking up, she rasped, "Andy, he's dead."

"But how? Are there any wounds? Blood?" he asked.

"Nothing I can see. Leslie, go back in the office. Call 9-1-1. Tell them we just discovered a body and to please send someone over." Leslie hurried back to the office area to place the call.

"Linda, look at this place," Andy said.

She had been so intent on examining Rick she hadn't noticed the room. Looking up, she gasped, "Andy, what in the name of God happened here?"

"I don't know. Maybe he had a seizure. The cart with your laptop and monitoring equipment is turned over. Everything on the counter is scattered all over the floor. Maybe he was fighting with someone."

"Rick wasn't due to start work for another twenty minutes. This ... whatever this is ... had to have happened several hours ago. His whole body is stiffening ... rigor mortis is setting in."

Chapter 2

———

DETECTIVE DAVID MILHOUS lived a few miles from the center of town on a rural road—perfect for morning jogs with his dog Whiskey. This morning, as usual, Whiskey's wet nose persistently nuzzled her master sprawled on top of the sheets. "Not yet, girl. Come on. Give me a few more minutes."

The Golden Retriever mix that David rescued from the local pound, sat down but both front paws landed on the bed with a thud along with a soft whine urging her master to get up. David opened his eyes a crack and was hit with the rays of a bright light streaming through his bedroom window as a tip of the sun rose above the horizon.

"Okay, Whiskey. I hear you."

The dog stood patiently by the bedroom door, tail wagging in anticipation for the best part of her day—the two of them on their morning, four-mile run. David lethargically pulled on his black jogging shorts and tank top. Moving a little faster, he slipped into his running shoes and gave the dog's silky head a pat letting her know it was almost time to go outside. Lifting her leash off the peg and grabbing an icy bottle of water from the refrigerator, he walked out on the deck that skirted his A-frame. Performing a few knee bends and head rolls, David snapped the leash on Whiskey's collar and took the few steps down to the gravel path that led to his driveway, his dog jumping off the deck to join him. They walked up the long driveway bordered on each side by rich vegetation of palms, pines, and live-oak trees adorned with thick Spanish moss. At the end of the cement driveway, they turned left onto the narrow, rural road and began a slow jog.

David, a six-foot tall hardened body, had just turned forty. His brown hair cropped short as befitting his position as lead detective for the Ocala Police Department, Criminal Investigation

Division, more commonly known as CID. He enjoyed his morning routine with his best friend. However, it wasn't just the mornings they spent together, Whiskey was always by his side. She sat next to him wherever he went—his black SUV, or a squad car, or on her blanket next to the detective's desk.

Now at the two-mile mark, David jogged faster. Whiskey kept turning her head sensing something behind them. She finally stopped dead in her tracks, turned around, and gave a soft bark, her tail wagging. David had to stop because the dog was not about to continue. David turned to see what was bothering his pooch and instantly smiled. A red-haired woman was jogging toward them dressed in white shorts and a halter top and holding a leash attached to a black and white Border Collie mix.

"Hi, mister," the woman said, pulling to a halt as the dogs sniffed around each other, tails wagging.

"Hello, yourself," David said. "If you're going further, how about we keep jogging?"

"Sure. I was about to turn around to head back, but Maggie and I are up to continuing on especially since she has a new friend. What's your dog's name?"

"This is Whiskey."

"Nice, given her coloring."

David and the woman began to jog again, each dog obediently slipping against the left-side of her master. David didn't start out at his original pace, deferring to the woman, but soon realized he'd better step it up as she began pulling away from him.

Now mile three the lady said, "I'll leave you here, have to head back. Nice running with you and Whiskey."

"Same here. Bye."

The woman, with Maggie in tow, turned and headed in the opposite direction.

David and Whiskey continued down the road. The dog looked up at him, tongue hanging out, and gave a soft whine.

"I know you have a new friend. The woman wasn't bad either. Wouldn't mind jogging with her again."

At the sound of his cell phone, he stopped to answer seeing it was from the department.

"Yah, Milhous here."

"Detective, we just had a 9-1-1 call from the Turner Equine Reproduction Center. Seems they found the body of their intern, a male, just a kid about twenty. The EMT unit is on the way. The caller said she didn't know what happened. Do you want to stop by the center on your way in?"

"Okay. I'll grab a quick shower and head over. They're only a couple of miles away. I'll check in with you after I see what's up."

Chapter 3

———

LINDA STOOD STARING down at their intern. Her mind raced trying to come up with some reason as to what had happened to the young man.

"Should we move him?" Andy asked.

"No. Don't touch a thing." Linda walked from one side of the body to the other, maintaining a three-foot distance.

Andy squatted down to get a better look at Rick's face. "Do you think he was doing drugs?"

"I don't think so, and if he was, why did he come here way before he was scheduled to work this morning?"

Their thoughts were interrupted with the sound of car doors slamming. The buzzer alerted them that someone had entered the building. Voices bounced off the walls of the sign-in area. Two paramedics, a man and a woman dressed in uniform, white shirts and black trousers, preceded Leslie into the examination room. Each carried a medical kit, immediately stepping to the body.

"I'm Brian and this is Ann," the man said as they both knelt down on either side of the body. "Are you Mr. and Mrs. Turner?" Brian asked without looking up.

"Yes," Andy replied. He and Linda moved out of their way.

"Mrs. Turner, did you call 9-1-1?" Ann asked.

"No, I asked Leslie to place the call as soon as we saw Rick," Linda replied, nodding toward Leslie as she spoke.

Brian rocked back on his heels. "There's no reviving him," he said closing his case. "This man's been dead a while. "Ann, please call the Medical Examiner to come pick him up while I pack away our equipment in the van." Brian looked up at Linda, "Because of his age the ME will probably perform an autopsy. It's standard procedure. I can't tell by looking at him what caused his death."

The front door buzzer sounded again and an officer walked into the examination room. "Ah, David, glad you could make it," Brian said. "Let me introduce you. Mr. and Mrs. Turner, this is Detective David Milhous, Ocala Police Department."

David shook hands with the Turners, his eyes darting around the room. "What do you think happened, Mrs. Turner?"

"We don't know. Leslie, our office manager you met on your way in, called me on my cell when she discovered Rick's body."

"Ann called the ME," Brian said to David. "Dr. Grant should be here soon. He asked us to wait to give him a hand."

"What's the boy's name?" David asked turning from Brian back to Linda.

"Richard Thurmond. He's been with us for about two months fulfilling an intern assignment for his veterinarian degree at the University of Florida," Linda said.

"Looks like a real struggle of some kind—stuff all over the place ... did you touch anything?" the detective asked.

"No," Linda said, "other than trying to roll him over to check if he was breathing. I was going to start CPR, but—"

"When did he usually arrive for work?" David asked.

"That's just it," Andy said. "He was way early—Linda thinks he's been dead a while. Leslie opens up at 8:30, and Linda received her call just before nine. We rushed right over."

"How did he get in ... did he have a key?"

"Yes, we gave him a key to the front door," Andy said. "Once in a while he arrived a little early to do some field work for his studies. The conference room is off the reception area. There are lots of medical publications on horses in the bookcases so he liked to work on his papers in there when he had a chance. He was a nice kid—thoughtful, respectful. We trusted him, didn't we, Linda."

"Yes, but your question about the key ... Leslie," Linda turned to Leslie standing in the doorway unable to take her eyes off the body. "Was the door unlocked when you came in this morning?"

"The front door was locked, but now that you ask, when I put the key in the door for the exam room it was unlocked. I thought maybe you were in the lab. That's when I found Rick."

"The lab?" David asked looking at Linda.

"Yes, the door behind you leads to our lab. We process the embryos, semen, and blood work in there."

"There's only one car parked outside. Is that yours, Leslie?"

"Yes, Detective."

"Did Rick live on the property, Mrs. Turner?"

"It's Linda, and my husband's name is Andy, and no, he didn't live here. He's renting a mobile home for the summer in a park about a mile from here. He has a car but generally rode his bike to work. Leslie, would you take a look. See if Rick's bike is where he usually stands it against the fence."

"Where does this door lead?" David asked.

Andy opened the door to the barn and he and the detective entered. The horses looked at their visitors and continued munching on the hay. "The horses due for an exam or requiring treatment are held in these stalls."

David walked out the back of the barn through the large, sliding barn door Andy had opened earlier. He walked a few feet out into the yard and returned just as a short, gray-haired gentleman with chiseled cheeks and thick horn-rimmed glasses entered the examination room.

Ann, standing watch over the body, greeted the man. "Hi, Alex. Let me introduce you to the Turners, Linda and Andy. They own this business." She looked at the Turners. "This is Dr. Alex Grant, Marion County Medical Examiner."

Linda and Andy shook the ME's hand. "Nice to meet you," Andy said, "but not under these circumstances."

"Alex," David said, "as you can see from the looks of this room something nasty happened here. It may be a case of a drug overdose. Nothing seems to be disturbed in the rest of the building—is that right, Linda?"

"I haven't really checked thoroughly, but right now I'd have to agree with you."

"I'll send some forensic officers over here, and also to where he was living. I'll need his address."

"Can they make it soon so we can clean the room up?" Linda asked.

"Of course. They should be here within the hour. Are you aware of any trouble the boy was in? Dealing drugs maybe?"

"As I said before," Andy replied, "he seemed to be a nice kid, good student, highly recommended by the school."

———

THE MEDICAL EXAMINER, with Brian and Ann's help, transferred the body to a body bag, then onto a gurney, and out to the wagon for transport to the morgue. David picked up the intern's address from Leslie and then called the department making arrangements for the forensic team to look around and gather evidence, as well as dusting for prints. He told them he would meet them later at the mobile home. He also told Linda and Andy he would be in touch as soon as Dr. Grant determined the cause of death, and after he had a chance to debrief the forensic officers.

David left the building and untied Whiskey from the fence post on his way to his car. She gave him a kiss and jumped into the SUV scooting over to the passenger seat. Linda and Andy stood in the entrance to the building watching the vehicles pull out of the driveway.

"Andy," Linda cried out, racing through the office area into the examination room. She pulled up short at a metal door in the white, cement-block wall punching in the key code. Darting through the door, she scanned the laboratory. Nothing was disturbed. She opened the refrigeration unit and then the freezer. All was in order.

"Linda, what is it?" Andy said following his wife into the lab.

"I just had a horrible thought that someone might have been after the semen we have stored here. Andy, it's our whole business—the trust the owners have placed in us to safeguard thousands of dollars worth of semen collections from their stallions."

"Don't worry, Linda. The way you have this lab protected, no one could get in without us knowing about it."

Chapter 4

JERRY STEVENS STOOD looking out his den window at his beautiful stallion, Black Magic. The two-and-a-half years old Arabian pranced around the paddock, tail flagging, mane flipping, in rhythm with his dance. Jerry could never get enough of the spectacular horse—his shiny black coat, jet-black mane and erect tail. But it was his conformation—the arch of his neck, and the big brown eyes that set him apart from other Arabians. He was in a class by himself.

Jerry was reliving Black Magic's performance in the ring at the regional show in Atlanta, where he became the Arabian Region XII Champion. Garnering this status was a big deal because the region has the largest membership of any of the regions, encompassing the states from North Carolina to Florida and from Tennessee to Mississippi on the Gulf Coast. But more important he was now eligible for the Arabian U.S. National show to be held in Albuquerque this October.

Black Magic's instant fame catapulted the Stevens Arabian Horse Farm into a million-dollar enterprise by virtue of his potential breeding fees. Stevens knew he needed some quick advice because of what he envisioned was coming with Black Magic at the national show. He had invited his investment manager Joe Rockwell, known as Rocket, to a meeting about the financial setup for his plans to expand the farm's business.

Rocket, on the other hand, was trying to pull his investment company back from the dead after his partner swindled him out of all his money. Framed for embezzlement, Joe had been sent to prison for a year and a half. Rocket, the name his business associates tagged him with because their portfolios rocketed up in earnings, was slowly clawing his way back into his former client's good graces. Jerry Stevens was one of those former clients, one who listened to Rocket and followed his advice to the letter. Arabian horses were Jerry's passion but he left the financial part to Rocket who had never let him down.

"So how big is this expansion you're talking about?" Joe asked.

"What? Oh, sorry, Joe, I checked out there for a minute. Barbara and I are still dazed by what's happened since the regional show. I'm already getting calls from owners who saw Magic in Atlanta. Joe, I wish you could have been there." Stevens turned again to the window. He didn't see the paddock in the brilliant sunlight—he was back at the show.

"When I entered the ring with Magic under halter, prancing him in front of the judges, and then around the ring, you could have heard a pin drop on the roughed-up dirt. That's how still the spectators were. When he stood up, posing in front of the judges—his graceful neck arched, leaning forward, hind legs straight, strong, and squarely underneath his body—soft oohs and aahs came from the stands. And then, when he was declared the champion, they rose to their feet and cheered as I led him around the ring again. He was amazing. Driving the trailer home that night, Barbara called me on my cell telling me about the owners, trainers and dealers who wanted to be put on the list for breeding services to their mares. The next day, there were even more calls—by evening we had tallied 250 requests for information. Out of that we should have a full book."

"Full book?"

"We're supposed to limit the number of contracts for stud services, for a single stallion, to 160 per year with AI—artificial insemination."

"Have you figured out the cost to fill a contract?" Rocket asked.

"That's just it. Barbara and I had to do some fast calculations. How much do breeders pay in advance to hold their place in line? Under what kind of agreement do we return a deposit? How long do the buyers have to register a new foal—it can be a couple of years from the time the breeding fee is collected, and the mare is inseminated until she has her foal. Then comes the registration, but the owner may still delay. They're lining up for semen—cooled and frozen. That's one reason why I need a bigger lab, to prepare the collections for shipment, but also to freeze the semen into straws for later sales."

"Are you going to start inseminating mares here on the farm?" Rocket asked looking at the spreadsheets Jerry had printed. He was trying to get a handle on the magnitude of Jerry's vision.

"No. I'm asking Linda Turner, you know the Equine Reproduction Center on the outskirts of Ocala, to handle that. Actually it's not far from here. She and her husband run an honest business and she is a terrific vet."

Jerry looked up as the door swung open, and Barbara entered carrying a tray laden with cream, sugar, chocolate-chip cookies, and a stainless-steel carafe.

"Thought you two might be ready for a fresh cup of coffee. Did I just hear you mention Linda's name?" Barbara asked, filling the empty mugs in front of each man.

"You did, and yes, I for one could use some more coffee," Jerry said, taking a sip of the piping hot liquid.

"Me, too, Barbara," Rocket chimed in. "This guy makes my head spin with all his plans—another stable, bigger lab. Black Magic's soon going to have offspring around the globe from the looks of it."

"I know what you mean. I get so excited as he lays it out in front of me," Barbara said, sitting on an arm of the couch, looking over at the stack of papers Joe had spread out on the desk. "Jerry, the reason I asked if you were talking about Linda is because she called while I was brewing your coffee. Seems her intern turned up dead in their examination room yesterday morning."

"What? That young kid?"

"Yes. The paramedics came but there was no reviving him. Then a detective arrived. The medical examiner picked up the body to take it to the morgue. Linda isn't sure of the cause of death. She hopes she'll hear from the ME before the end of the day, or tomorrow at the latest."

Jerry slumped down in the brown leather recliner facing the picture window and the pastures beyond. He leaned forward, holding the coffee mug with both hands. His head dropped as he gazed at the steam rising from the mug.

"Jerry, I know what you're thinking, but this is just an act of God. Nothing more," Barbara said.

"Ah, I think I'm missing something here," Rocket said. "Is there something going on? Something you two are worried about?"

"I don't know, Joe. Linda mentioned a couple of strange events in passing the other day, and I've had some fencing knocked over." Jerry rubbed his scalp a couple of times and then took another sip of coffee.

"Jerry, nothing that can't be explained," Barbara said placing her hand on her husband's shoulder.

"Well, folks, given my recent bout with the law and the stories I heard while I took that little vacation in prison, I know that things seemingly random can sometimes fit into a bigger picture. I suggest you have a chat with Linda and plug in with that detective she met."

Chapter 5

———

AT THE OCALA PD AN officer was booking a thirty-something, surly DUI. Upstairs, David sat tapping his pen on the calendar pad that supposedly helped to preserve the desk's surface from spilled coffee, but in reality served as the target for his mindless doodles as he pondered the death at the equine center. Whiskey was asleep on her blanket next to her master's desk. Leaning forward, the detective punched the blinking white light on his telephone console signaling an incoming call.

"Milhous."

"Hi, David, I have the preliminary results regarding the young lad we brought in from the equine center," the medical examiner said.

"I was about to call you, Alex. I didn't want the end of the week to get here without knowing how the kid died. Whatcha got for me?"

"He seems to have had a dose of cocaine, crack really—but what we found in his blood shouldn't have been enough to kill him. We'll know more after the autopsy, but that won't be until next week."

"How do you think he took the drug? Injection? Freebasing?" David asked adding more squiggles to his masterpiece on the desk pad.

"There are no needle marks, at least nothing we could find with a cursory examination. As I said, we found the drug in a blood sample."

"Any other marks on his body?"

"A couple of bruises on both of his upper arms. I suppose there would be many occasions while tending the horses that he could have sustained such trauma, and then there's the additional chaos to the equipment and other paraphernalia at the scene.

There was another spot on his chest, but I'm not ready to say what caused it."

"When do you peg the time of death?"

"Rigor had set in. I would say it was sometime in the early morning, say between two and four a.m."

"Alex, I didn't have a chance to check his pockets. Was he carrying anything—wallet, keys?"

"Yes. The only things on his person were his clothes and keys in his pocket."

"Okay. Send over your report and, Alex, take his fingerprints and upload them to the central database. Email me his case number."

"Will do but it will be preliminary. I'm ordering up a more extensive drug screen. Anything else?" Dr. Grant asked.

"That's it for now. I'll be talking with Linda Turner to see what her plans are for the body. I presume the kid must have family somewhere. I'll talk to them—certainly do want to ask them a few questions."

David retrieved the Turner's business card from his pocket and tapped in their number. Leslie picked up the phone, dropped it, and then retrieved it from the floor.

"Hi, this is Detective Milhous. Is Andy or Linda around?"

"Hi, Detective, I'm a little edgy I guess. Both Linda and Andy are examining a mare. I'll ask Linda to call you back. Hold on a minute ... she just came in."

David caught some bits and pieces of conversation and then Linda came on the line. "Hi, Detective. I hope you have some information for us."

"Good morning, Linda. Yes, I just spoke with Alex, Dr. Grant, the ME you met. Rick came up positive with cocaine in his blood. Dr. Grant believes it was crack. I know you told me Rick didn't do drugs, but has anything come to mind since we talked?"

"No. Andy and I checked him out before we accepted him as an intern. He came highly recommended. He was in the top percentile of his class. I just can't see him taking drugs of any kind."

"Well, he had cocaine that night. Dr. Grant said he'd been dead about four or five hours by the time Leslie found him. Also, he did have keys on him. Linda, how would he gain entrance to the examination room?"

"He had to come through two doors—the front entrance to the center, then the door into the exam room. He had the keys, one for each, that opened both of those doors—sometimes he beat Leslie into work. I told you, he was very diligent about his reports both for us and for his professors."

"How about coming in through the other direction? That big sliding barn door at the other end of the stalls—I walked out to the grassy area yesterday to take a look around."

"There's a padlocked gate next to the side of our building, and then the sliding door you mentioned has a padlock. Only Andy and I have that key. We're pretty tight."

"Was Leslie the first one in Monday?"

"Yes, she arrives close to 8:30 and opens the three doors at nine—front entrance, examination room, and stall area. I'll ask her, but I'm sure she would have mentioned if either of them was unlocked. She ... wait a minute. She did say the door into the exam room was unlocked, but everything else seemed normal until she saw Rick."

"Does he have family in the area?"

"I pulled out his employment form from our files. His parents live in Atlanta. I called them shortly after you left. Naturally, they're devastated—their only son. They'll be on their way down to Ocala soon. They weren't very coherent when I talked with them, you know, about arrangements. I expect to meet them tomorrow or Saturday. Should they contact you or the medical examiner?"

"I'd like you to have them call me. I'll meet them somewhere, at your center if it's okay with you. I want to ask them some questions about their son's friends, habits, and so on."

"You are definitely welcome here. Drugs are the last thing I would have expected as having anything to do with his death."

Chapter 6

"GOOD MORNING TO YOU all out there. This is channel 13 morning news at nine. As you just heard from Katy, she predicts that afternoon showers will provide some relief from the past five days of high temperatures and humidity.

Late last night we received word from the Ocala Police Department of the death of a young veterinarian intern discovered at the Turner Equine Reproduction Center Monday morning. The center is located on the western outskirts of Ocala. Sources tell us drugs may have been involved. The police are waiting for the medical examiner's autopsy report before releasing how and why this young man died.

The deceased is reportedly Richard Thurmond from Atlanta. He was a student at the University of Florida in Gainesville. After the completion of this summer's internship requirement, Mr. Thurmond was scheduled to graduate next spring.

Dr. Linda Turner, the owner and veterinarian of the equine center, and her husband Andrew Turner were unavailable for comment. The police liaison said the Turners are expected to meet with the intern's parents sometime this weekend."

"WHAT HAPPENED? This was supposed to be a slam dunk."

"Yep, well, at first he seemed okay—with a little persuasion that is. Then he started to get cold feet, panicked. I had to get out quick."

"You stupid ass—a simple petty theft job and you murder the guy!"

Chapter 7

———

AT SIX O'CLOCK SATURDAY morning the temperature held at eighty degrees dropping from the high of ninety-eight the previous day. David and Whiskey were already out jogging—partly to beat the heat and partly because he was concentrating on the questions he was going to ask Rick Thurmond's parents. Whiskey suddenly halted, turned around and sat down on the asphalt, her tail sweeping the pine needles.

David, feeling the slack in the leash tighten, turned to see why his friend wasn't moving. A few yards back the lady he met Monday morning and her dog Maggie were approaching at a fast clip.

The woman came up alongside Whiskey and stopped, her breathing only slightly elevated. "Hello, Whiskey. Yes, yes, you're a pretty girl," she said accepting a slurp on her cheek.

Maggie and Whiskey then took to greeting each other.

"Hello, there. If we're going to keep meeting like this I guess we should introduce ourselves. My name is David." Smiling he extended his hand to her.

Wiping the moisture off her palm onto her red shorts, Elizabeth returned the smile and took his hand. "I'm Liz. Nice to meet you. I swear Maggie saw Whiskey long before I did. She's been pulling me along since I left the house."

"Then I guess, Liz, we best run off some of her energy."

The foursome once again began pounding down the road, Liz's red ponytail swaying as the dogs resumed their place on the left side of their respective masters. David and Liz chatted about the neighborhood, the weather, and the heat. This time it was David who cut his jog short, explaining he had to get to work. "Nice to meet you, Liz. Maybe we'll hook up again tomorrow."

"Have a nice day, David. Bye." She and Maggie continued on.

———

RETURNING TO HER RENTAL HOUSE, a nice little bungalow tucked back in the pine and live-oak trees and sheltered by overgrown vegetation, Liz filled Maggie's bowl with Kibbles and headed for the shower. Humming, she dressed in her signature PI costume: white shirt with starched pointed collar, sleeves short or long depending on the weather; black leather shoes with crepe soles, peeked out from under the black straight-legged slacks. Today her shoulder-length hair curved under her chin. She returned to the kitchen and fixed herself a peanut butter and jelly sandwich, retrieved two bottles of water from the refrigerator, and headed out to the car, Maggie at her heels.

Liz pulled in behind a two-story strip mall, a scant five miles from where she lived, and parked her car. The building looked like something from New Orleans' Bourbon Street. The cement block was painted a light gray. White wrought-iron railings with a fancy filigree design every other foot outlined the second floor balcony as well as the stairs at either end of the building. Pillars constructed of matching wrought iron stood between each business on the ground floor and supported the balcony above.

A florist and a laundromat were located on the street level with several vacancies interspersed. Liz and a realtor were the only two renters on the second level. The balcony was open to the elements but protected by an overhang and the white railing. A friend had emailed her that she was leaving for California. If Liz wanted to start her business in Ocala, she could pick up the lease on the office space as well as the little house she was renting. Liz jumped to accept both deals and the landlords were delighted with the arrangement.

Liz strode through the tunnel, which connected the rear parking lot to the front of the building, and up the staircase to the second floor. Her hands full with her lunch, water bottles, shoulder bag, and the end of Maggie's leash, she fumbled with the keys and finally found the one she wanted.

Entering the small, one-room office, Liz flipped on the AC, unsnapped Maggie's leash, and set everything on her desk, including her laptop computer. The room was sparsely furnished—a dented file cabinet in the corner, a heavy oak door resting on two black-metal file cabinets served as a desk on which sat a desk lamp—a pink flamingo adorned with a pale-blue lampshade. Two straight-back chairs were carefully placed in front of the desk for clients. She had splurged on a second-hand wicker plant stand which she positioned by the front entrance to soften the space. There was a closet which doubled as a restroom complete with toilet and sink. The landlord had spruced-up the walls with a fresh coat of lime-green paint. The walls of the office area matched the restroom.

Liz thought the setup was wonderful.

This was her first office. After spending two years at Goodwurthy Detective Agency learning the ins and outs of running an investigative business, and serving his clients, she had given her notice and set out to establish her own business as a private investigator. Goodwurthy was sorry to lose the woman who had quickly become his star agent. He had given her two of his on-going clients in the Ocala area as a present when she left, plus announced he would send clients her way when he was overloaded.

"Well, Maggie, we aren't exactly setting the private investigation business on fire. I was hoping our ad in the newspaper might at least lead to a couple of phone calls."

Maggie answered with a thump of her tail but didn't raise her head. The dog had dragged her large pillow from the corner to the center of the room and flopped down on it. She was tuckered out from her morning jog.

It was now the end of her first week. If anyone had seen her ad in the West Marion Messenger, the community newspaper, they certainly hadn't felt the need to call. Liz took her seat behind her desk and looked at the silent phone. As if by her sheer will to make the black instrument ring—it rang. Startled, she jumped up knocking over her chair. Grabbing the phone for fear the caller might hang up, she answered in her most professional voice, "Stitchway, Private Investigator, may I help you?"

"Hi, Lizzy. Just wanted to congratulate you on your first week. Mom and I are driving your way and thought we might stop off for a visit after you finish work. Your mom's been cooking up a storm—how does a home-cooked meal sound? We'll bring all the fixins."

"Dad, you scared me. At least I know the phone works, and yes, home-cooked food sounds great. How about five-after-five?" she asked, giggling.

"That's just fine. See you then, pumpkin."

Liz pulled her chair back up on its legs, and once again sat down. She moved the phone to the center of the desk, placed her new yellow-lined tablet a little to the left with a pen and pencil alongside. She stood up to freshen Maggie's water bowl when the phone rang.

It's probably dad again, she thought. Wants me to pick something up on my way home for dinner. "Hello, Stitchway, PI."

"Is this Stitchway Private Investigators?"

"Yes, yes, it is." Elizabeth scooted around to the back of her desk, leaned over and picked up her pen. Settling on the chair, she pulled the yellow tablet toward her.

"I'd like to talk to you about a possible job. It's probably nothing, but we may be too close to a situation. We need a fresh pair of eyes. Would you be available sometime today?"

"Of course, I'm sure we can agree on a time. Your name please?"

"Well, first, I trust if we do come to an understanding it would be strictly on a confidential basis."

"Absolutely. If there is one thing Stitchway Investigation prides itself on its confidentiality. We work with the utmost discretion, Ms.—"

"Turner, Linda Turner. By any chance could you stop by this morning, say, eleven?"

"Yes, Ms. Turner. The address?"

"Turner Equine Reproduction Center, turn right onto Route 225 off of Route 40." Liz wrote the address and directions down on her tablet.

"I'll see you at eleven." Liz hung up the phone and began dancing around the room. She sang out, "A client, Maggie, a client."

Maggie jumped up and joined in the new game, barking at her mistress jumping around in front of her.

Chapter 8

————

AS LIZ ENTERED THE APPOINTMENT with Mrs. Turner into her computer her fingers paused over the keyboard. She had heard something about the equine center on the news. Then she remembered—earlier this week there had been a report about a body being discovered there. *I wonder if that has something to do with the call,* she thought. She turned off her laptop and picked up her briefcase. Giving Maggie a pat on the head, she locked the office door and ran down the stairs to her car. After giving some thought recently she had decided to trade in her fun, yellow Ford coupe for a second-hand, silver-gray Taurus sedan. With a smile on her face, she was on her way to meet her first client.

Turning off the highway onto a rural road, Liz took note of the increasing foliage interrupted now and then with lush green pastures. The car's AC was turned on high but the radio was off. Not knowing why Mrs. Turner wanted to meet with her, she could only surmise it had something to do with the body. She couldn't make a list of questions, but her antenna was up for any eventuality.

Spotting the equine center's sign, she pulled off the asphalt road onto a circular gravel driveway. Fencing skirted the outer edge of the driveway connecting to a low, one-story building. Liz parked off to the side under the shade of a large live oak dripping with moss. Picking up her briefcase from the seat next to her, she climbed out of the car but immediately stopped in her tracks.

In front of her, attached to the left-hand side of the building was a paddock. A baby filly was prancing around, dashing in one direction then another, kicking its heels up as she did so. The mother stood to the side quietly looking over the weathered, wooden fence to the pasture beyond. Liz was mesmerized by the beauty of the foal. Not really knowing, she guessed it was an Arabian given the conformation of her body and tapered ankles.

Shaking her head she walked up to the front door and let herself into the building. She was greeted by a young woman sitting at the desk.

"Hi, I'm here to see Mrs. Turner. I believe she's expecting me."

"Hello. I'm Leslie. Dr. Turner did tell me to be on the lookout for an eleven o'clock appointment, Miss ..."

"Stitchway, Elizabeth Stitchway."

"I'm Leslie," the woman said with a broad smile. "I'll let Linda know you're here."

"Thank you." Liz walked around the small space. A door was open opposite the reception desk. She looked inside at what appeared to be a conference room—large rectangular, slightly worn table in the center, windows on two sides with bookcases facing the windows. Liz heard a door open to her right and a pretty, blue-eyed blonde, hair pulled back in a ponytail, entered with a surge of energy and engaging smile. Liz thought she was probably in her late thirties, maybe forty.

Linda walked up to her, hand extended. "Miss Stitchway, thank you for being so prompt. Let's go into the conference room. Leslie, call Andy will you? Tell him Miss Stitchway is here." Linda turned back to Liz and led her into the conference room. Indicating a chair for Liz, they both sat down.

"You're probably wondering why I called you. Did you hear the news this week about a body we found at our center—"

Linda was interrupted as Andy entered the room closing the door behind him. Not a tall man, five-foot-ten, slim, dark hair topped with a baseball cap, wearing a green shirt over jeans pushed down into black rubber boots.

"Sorry, I just let Sinbad out into the back pasture," he said to his wife.

"Andy, this is Miss Stitchway."

"Liz, please call me Liz. Nice to meet you, Andy." Liz stood to shake his hand.

"And please call me Linda." She smiled as Andy joined the women at the conference table. "I was just about to fill Liz in on why I asked her to come over," Linda said turning away from her husband and back to Liz. "It's about our intern. Leslie found his body Monday morning but nothing seems to add up as to what happened."

"I heard on the news that he was taken to the morgue. What did the medical examiner say caused his death?" Liz asked.

"He didn't know for sure but said he had cocaine in his blood. He's doing more testing. I didn't talk to him directly. Detective Milhous called to give us the update."

"What's the intern's name?" Liz asked, retrieving a notepad and pen from her briefcase.

"Rick Thurmond. His parents are coming down from Atlanta this weekend and the detective wants to meet with them."

"Did Rick have a drug problem?"

"No, no, I'm sure he didn't," Andy said. "He came highly recommended from the University of Florida. He had interned with us the past two summers."

"He was very methodical about his work," Linda interjected. "Kept lengthy records and was always writing reports for us as well as papers to be turned in fulfilling his intern assignments."

"Were there any needle marks on his arm?"

"Not that I was told about, and I never saw any."

"What did the ME say about the time of death?"

"He said he'd been dead about six hours and thought he died sometime between two and four in the morning ... but Andy and I can't figure out why he was in the building. Rick had rented a mobile home a mile or two from here and generally rode his bike to work."

"Did you find his bike?"

"No. I tell you, Liz, there are so many things that aren't adding up." Both Linda and Andy leaned forward over the table, hands folded in front of them, looking intently at Liz.

"Can you show me where Leslie found him?"

"Sure. Andy, can you see if that new kid we hired knows where to put the feed hay, while I show Liz around?"

"Yea. Catch you later, Liz. Hope you can help bring some clarity to Rick's death."

Andy shook Liz's hand and left. Linda followed her husband out the door indicating that Liz should come with her. They walked past the reception desk, through a door, and entered a large room. A stall surrounded by metal rails and a gate on each end was off to the right. A cart was positioned next to it. Opposite the cart was a large barrel with a black garbage bag lining the inside. Cabinets with countertops bordered the walls to the left.

"This is the examination room. We do most of our work here which is between the lobby area and the barn." Linda opened the door to the barn. "The stalls you see are where the horses scheduled for treatment are held."

Turning away from the barn door, Linda stepped back into the exam area. Liz followed taking in the aroma of the hay made more pungent by the high humidity filling the barn. "Andy will bring a mare in to be examined. She's led into this stock and the gate is closed behind her. Andy stays with her, holding onto the halter lead, while I do the exam on the other end," Linda said with a little smile.

"Rick was curled up here in the middle of the floor. I rolled him over but couldn't lay him on his back—my first thought was to administer CPR."

"I take it he wasn't breathing."

"No. I checked and that's when I saw his eyes—open and staring into space."

"Was anything disturbed in the room?"

"Disturbed isn't the word for it. It was a mess. It was as if he fought with someone. Anything on the counter was strewn on the floor. That cart you see with my laptop was turned over. Fortunately, the computer is okay."

"If not a fight, maybe a seizure of some kind?"

"You know, Liz, that possibility came to my mind as well." Linda turned to her right and punched in a code on the outside of a door. At the sound of the latch releasing she opened the door into her laboratory.

"We perform many procedures on the horses that are brought to us. The one we do the most is the insemination of a mare with cooled or frozen sperm sent to us from all over the world. We also can flush a pregnant mare's embryo and place it into a recipient mare."

"Whoa. You lost me. Cooled, frozen, recipient mares ... help me out here." Liz smiled looking at Linda with raised brows.

"Sorry, I slipped into my professorial jargon," Linda said laughing. "Breeding rarely takes place the old-fashioned way especially where Arabs are concerned."

"Arabs?"

"Sorry. In the horse world, Arabian horses are very often referred to as Arabs. Let's go outside and I'll walk you through what we do—the process."

Linda led Liz through the barn and out to the grassy area in back. Looking to her right, she pointed to another small barn with three stalls about twenty yards away.

"See that high bench over there by the stalls. Picture it as a mare's back and rump. That's called a phantom mare. We put a couple of mares in heat in those stalls. Andy brings the stallion over. He gets excited and climbs onto the phantom. The phantom can be adjusted to the stallion's height."

"Slick," Liz said staring at the apparatus.

"Yes, and much safer for the horses. No fear of injuries."

"What about the collection—that's a word I've heard."

"Well, after the stallion mounts the phantom, mind you Andy guides him to the phantom and holds onto the halter, I attach a collection tube to the stallion and the stream goes into a canister which I'll be holding. Let's walk back to the lab."

Liz followed Linda, looking back at the little barn and the phantom, with the picture in her mind that Linda had drawn.

"Once we collect the semen, we take a look at a sample under the microscope to determine the stallion's sperm count. One of our client's stallions, Black Magic for instance, is very fertile. He has a high sperm count. Then depending on if the semen is going to be cooled or frozen, or both, we prepare it for shipment, or storage, or insemination if the mare is already at our facility."

"Okay, but you said something about flushing the mare."

"Let's say I inseminate a mare and it takes—I can flush that embryo from the donor and transfer it into a recipient mare. If we did nothing, she'll have her foal in eleven months. On the other hand, maybe the owner wants to continue to show her, or she's old and it might be dangerous for her if she tried to give birth. But she's a champion and an owner wants to breed her with a champion stallion. In which case, I flush out the embryo. Now, the only way we know if we got it is through a microscope. When I find an embryo, I then place it in a recipient mare who carries it to term."

"Does the mare stay with you?"

"More often than not the owners who paid for the breeding trailer her to their farm. Once the foal is born, we go pick her up, or they bring her back."

"A lot of delicate procedures you perform here, Linda. Do you ever get called to other farms?"

"Yes. We are especially close to the Stevens Arabian Horse Farm, not too far from here."

"You punched a keypad to access your lab. Who knows the code?"

"Andy, of course, and Leslie, and Rick had the code. He sometimes prepared the equipment stored in here for the examinations."

"You mentioned frozen semen. I see refrigeration units in here. They have locks on them. Who has access to them?"

"Only Andy and I. When you get into frozen semen you're talking big bucks, and, of course, our integrity—ensuring that the correct semen is inseminated into the right mare or shipped to the buyer who paid for the breeding. You know, Liz, on the morning Rick was found, and after the ME had removed his body, I came in here ... Andy thinks I'm paranoid, but it felt strange. I checked everything carefully, but I swear something was out of place."

Chapter 9

RUSTY BURNS, FIVE-FEET-TEN-INCHES tall, toned body, was a high-spirited woman. She loved to laugh and have fun but could turn on a dime becoming shrill, conniving, her flaming red hair sending out sparks burning anyone around her. Her birth certificate showed her name as Rebecca. But when the red-haired, green-eyed baby girl made her appearance, Charles Burns jokingly called his baby daughter Rusty and it stuck.

The only child of her well-to-do parents, she grew up on the family farm nestled in the foothills of Canyon Creek located on the southern end of Black Canyon City, forty miles north of Phoenix, Arizona. Her parents, Charles and Henrietta, everyone called her Henry, lavished her with everything she asked for. As early as Rusty could remember she spent most of her hours in the barn, paddock, or pastures with the horses. She rode her pony, Patty, until her parents jokingly thought she had become one with the little filly.

Rusty will always remember her twenty-first birthday …

THE FAMILY OF THREE gathered in the living room under a cathedral ceiling that soared to the heavens. Creamy frosted birthday cake, picketed with twenty-one candles sat on the sideboard.

Yuma, a Navajo Indian, strolled in to join the celebration—carrying the scent of leather and fresh soap. His black hair with streaks of gray was pulled back in a ponytail.

"Sorry, if I'm late," he said.

"You're never late, my friend." Charles poured champagne into the crystal flutes aligned on the silver tray. "I just popped the cork." Passing the glasses filled with the bubbly to his wife, daughter, and friend, he then raised his flute to Rusty, "Happy birthday my little spitfire." He tapped his glass gently to hers.

"Happy birthday, dear," her mother said kissing her daughter's cheek.

"Happy birthday, Rusty," Yuma said, with an easy smile as he too touched his glass to hers.

Yuma, Navajo meaning son of a chief, was a natural with horses. He applied to manage the livestock on Charles Burns' new farm just after he purchased the property some twenty-one years ago. The Indian was an honorable man—didn't believe in gambling, cheating, or stealing from his employer. He didn't drink—his only vice was cigarettes. One day Charles introduced him to the cigar. From that day on the Cuban version became his holiday treat. Yuma quickly became part of the family and was given a small cottage to live in on the edge of a creek running alongside the farm.

"Thank you one and all," Rusty said, raising her glass in the air turning to gaze lovingly into the eyes of each in turn.

"Here, sweetheart, you must open this present first," her mother said.

"But, mom, it's too pretty." Rusty picked up the box, jiggled it from side to side, then placed it on her lap. Smiling and with a little shrug of her shoulders, she untied the wide yellow satin ribbon, and carefully removed the shiny orange wrapping paper. Taking the lid off, she pulled back the yellow tissue paper to reveal a fifteen-inch picture frame.

"Do you know what it is?" her father asked. The frame contained a greeting—Happy Birthday—in red letters on a royal-blue background.

"I believe I do. It's one of those computerized frames." She turned the frame over and pushed the button. The eight-by-ten-inch display came to life revealing a picture of a young girl on a pony. "It's me and Patty, my pony."

"You were only eleven, dear, but cute as a button with that mop of red hair." Her mother smiled at the picture of her young daughter.

Rusty put the frame on the large, carved-oak coffee table, polished to a glossy sheen. Her mother and father moved to sit beside her on the couch.

"Yuma, you took this picture, I think," Rusty said.

"That's right." Yuma moved behind the couch looking at the picture over the family's shoulders.

"Not a hard guess," Charles said. "Yuma's the only one who could figure out that digital camera. You groomed that pony until we had to put on sunglasses her coat was so shiny. You thought she was the most beautiful horse in the world."

Yuma leaned his elbows on the back of the couch. "You wanted to learn what you had to do to show her. Had to know as soon as I gave you a lift up to ride. It didn't take long before you entered her—there, that's a picture of your first show. Look at the next picture—you asleep outside her stall at the show."

"Everyone was so noisy," Rusty said, giggling. "I wanted to keep people away so she could rest. I remember being so afraid she would be tired and not do her best in the ring."

"And then, mercy me, you saw an Arabian," Henry said. We never heard the end of your pleading for such a horse until on your thirteenth birthday we gave you a purebred Arab mare."

The picture dissolved into one of Rusty leading a bay horse.

"When that mare came to live on the farm, you pestered Yuma unmercifully until he agreed to show you everything he knew about horses." Charles picked up the champagne bottle from the silver bucket and topped off everyone's glass. "I had to hire a part-time helper for Yuma because you monopolized his time. He was so patient teaching you about grooming and schooling the horses. But, he said you had to learn the other part of raising horses, too—the general care of our farm's horse family, but with particular attention to that new Arab mare."

"Is there a picture of her foal?" Rusty asked pushing the button to advance to the next frame. "There she is. She was such a lovely filly, pure Arab, too." Rusty flashed a smile back at Yuma.

"Yes. She was," Yuma replied. "I thought I could catch up with my other duties, but oh, no, you immediately wanted me to show you how to train the filly for the yearling competition. You had big dreams ... still do I might add."

"I know. I entered her in the Regional Class A. I had plans for that competition—I just knew she was going to qualify for the national show."

"From that point on you ate, drank, and talked of nothing else but horses, particularly Arabians," her mother added.

The picture dissolved to one of Rusty accepting the congratulations of a judge. Charles leaned forward to get a better look at the image. "When Yuma finally said it was time, you entered the filly and she took first in her class as a yearling. Do you remember that trainer who came to her stall after you won?"

"Dad, I'll never forget. He told me that I had a lot of talent. I wasn't exactly sure what that meant, but I knew it was good."

Another picture appeared of the trainer's farm. "You found yourself driving trucks and trailers as well as grooming his horses for a few years," Charles added.

Rusty and her dad laughed at the next picture of a young girl driving a truck—she could barely see out of the windshield.

"You were only fifteen, dear," Henry chimed in.

The images dissolved, one after the other. Pictures of when Rusty began showing other people's horses, working with horse traders in town, grooming and trading their horses for sale and shows.

A picture appeared of Rusty with a storm on her face going into her school.

"Oh, no, you included that pic. I remember that day. Boy, I didn't want to go to school, but you and dad insisted, adamant as I remember, about my getting good grades. But when I graduated from high school you let me go to work at a lady's farm for the summer. She was terrific—there's her picture. I learned so much from her. She had me showing her horses and I won several events. Then a few months after, a representative of the Arabian Horse Association asked me if I I'd like to be a youth judge, which opened up a whole new path. But I really preferred working with the horses."

"Yes, but then you soon were asked to judge at a regional event." Yuma said sipping the last of his champagne.

"I accepted the work but only if I didn't have a horse entered in the event. Showing a horse always came first," Rusty replied.

The frame had cycled back to the first picture of Rusty at eleven years old.

"So, Rusty," her father said, pouring the last of the champagne equally into their glasses, "Today is your twenty-first birthday. Your mother and I thought we'd ask you what you wanted for a present on this most special of days?"

Rusty jumped up from the couch and walked to the mammoth fireplace stacked with white logs. She turned to face her parents.

"I want to rename our farm. Burns Arabian Horse Ranch. And I want to manage it."

"What about Yuma?" her dad asked.

"Oh, he'll continue to run everything just like now," she said smiling at Yuma. "But I'll take over the Arabians. What do you think? Will you give me the one thing I want in the whole world?" She looked from her father to her mother and they looked at each other.

Yuma smiled. He knew what their answer would be.

Charles and Henrietta Burns had always had a hard time refusing their daughter anything since the day she made her appearance—a curly red-haired baby screaming like a banshee.

Charles raised his eyebrows seeking his wife's approval. Henry raised her eyebrows in return, tilted her head to one side, a big smile began to spread across her pretty face. The deal was sealed.

"That will be quite an undertaking, young lady. You know nothing about ranching, but I guess if Yuma gets to hang around to help, so can I." Her father popped another cork and filled everyone's champagne flutes, continuing the birthday celebration.

Rusty embraced her mother and father, and ran around the couch, giving Yuma a hug. Walking back to the fireplace she turned to face her family. "I'll raise the most beautiful Arabians. Of course, I want to show them, but most of all I want to become known as the person to see and the place to go for Arabian champions—to buy, to train, and to breed."

Chapter 10

―――

RUSTY ALWAYS SMILED WHEN she thought back on her twenty-first birthday, now ten years ago. Smiled remembering her response when her parents asked her what she wanted as a gift. To fulfill his daughter's wish, Charles had insisted on adding a wing to the house, a suite of rooms, giving Rusty privacy as well as an office for a growing business. The wing had its own back entrance—the barn only a few steps down the path. Theresa was hired to work full time, managing the care of the house and preparing the meals.

Brushing away her birthday ruminations, Rusty, grabbed the truck keys off the black granite countertop in the kitchen and headed out. Painted on the side of her red, super-duty Ford truck was a silver-gray Arabian horse with flowing black mane and tail. Underneath in shimmery silver letters was a sign that read: *Burns Arabian Horse Ranch, Grooming, Training, Breeding.*

Now thirty-one, she had done well in her efforts to make a mark for herself in Arabian horse circles. Her parents stocked the ranch in the first two years with five full-Arabian mares. All placed second or third in Class A Regional shows with Rusty showing them. Charles Burns went all out and purchased a champion stallion from Dubai. So far, Rusty had been blessed with several foals that looked promising. But, it was the training side of her business that had taken off. Not only was she training but also showing some of her client's horses. She picked up a percentage of their winnings, and their success brought more attention to her skills.

But she wanted more.

She was not satisfied with her progress, though realizing it would take time to build the clientele. Fame was her goal. Rusty was hoping her meeting today would produce a breakout championship. The owners of a yearling, full Arabian from championship stock, wanted to talk to her about training their filly to be a champion show horse. The stallion that had sired the foal lived on their ranch, which was located outside of Scottsdale in the shadows of Camelback Mountain.

Rusty drove south on Black Canyon Highway and then turned east onto Route 101. Following the Peterson's directions, she spotted the ranch and turned into the long driveway. She stopped in front of a large iron gate and pressed the buzzer on a stanchion beside her truck, as she had been instructed. The gate swung open.

Following the paved driveway, she circled around the large Spanish style home—stucco with a red tiled roof nestled in an abundance of colorful foundation bushes and flowers. As she passed the house she noticed a courtyard through a latticed iron gate. Looking ahead she caught sight of the barn surrounded by pastures, each fenced with white painted rails so the horses could be turned out yet kept separate at the same time. *Money's no object here,* she thought.

Rusty pulled up to the open entrance of a large barn and parked. She had been on the road a little over an hour. The summer heat was blistering and she pulled her cream-colored cowgirl hat down to shade her eyes as she climbed out of her truck. Feeling a bit stiff, Rusty raised her shoulders to stretch her back then tucked her white silk blouse neatly into her skinny jeans.

The Petersons immediately emerged from the side door of the barn, big smiles on their faces. Mrs. Peterson, a petite blonde in a white embroidered cotton shirt, tight jeans, and brown tooled boots, quickly walked out in front of her husband. Mr. Peterson towered over his wife by at least a foot, and his black-felt Stetson made him appear gigantic. Rusty put them both somewhere in their forties.

"Hello, I'm Rusty Burns and you must be Mrs. Peterson." Rusty extended her hand shaking hands with the Petersons in turn.

"Oh, my dear, we are so happy to finally meet you, aren't we, sweetheart? And please call me Sally, and he's Hank," Mrs. Peterson said looking back at her husband laughing.

"Yes, we are," Mr. Peterson said with a chuckle, joining his wife. "We think we have a winner but have no idea what to do about it."

Rusty liked the couple immediately and was anxious to see the yearling. Sally led the way into the barn and to the large stall where a mare stood peering out the stall door to see who was coming. Mr. Peterson told her the mare had placed first in several regional shows and had been a reserve champion as well. A filly was prancing around in the next stall. Hank followed his wife, and Rusty got the impression that whatever his wife did was fine with him. She seemed to wear the pants in the family. There had been no mention of children.

Rusty walked up to the stall and looked in at the filly. "She is a beauty. I can see why you're so excited."

"I named her Sunny after my wife," Hank said. "They are the sunshine of my life." Standing behind Sally, he wrapped his arms around her, giving her a peck on the neck.

"Oh, now, Hank, honestly Rusty doesn't want to hear such stuff."

Rusty, laughing in response to their byplay, moved to take a look at the mare. "I presume you're planning to keep breeding her, especially if Sunny places in a show. Potential horse dealers and owners would surely be interested in her sire as well."

"Yes, we thought that. Hank and I went to the National Arabian Horse show last year in Louisville, and we witnessed the excitement first hand. We overheard the dealers negotiating, and owners asking about breeding deals. Hank, put the halter on Sampson. Bring him out to the paddock so Rusty can get a good look at Sunny's daddy."

The three congregated shortly in a paddock to the side of the barn. Rusty spoke softly to the stallion taking her time with her approach—stroking his nose, neck, and back. She stepped away to get a good look at his conformation. She noticed something that could possibly keep him from a championship. She had never before suggested any surgical alteration to a horse to remove an imperfection. But this stallion was so superb to any other she had seen except for the one flaw. With the rapport that had developed between her and the Petersons, she thought they might agree to let her show the stallion at the next show, especially if she was training their foal, Sunny. Both horses would stay at her ranch.

"He is a remarkable animal. I would think you could command a nice breeding fee around the country which would also increase the filly's value. Has your vet ever said anything about him being a little thick through the throat, the throat latch?"

"Why, no," Sally said. "Has our vet mentioned anything like that to you, dear?"

"No. Show us what you mean, Rusty."

Rusty moved to the stallion's side and faced the Petersons. "See, here if I hold this fatty area of his throat up, look at the better line of his neck ... a small flaw ... but, yet—"

"Oh my," Sally said. "I do see how that would be an improvement. Do you think that's the reason he's never placed higher than third?"

"Could be."

"What exactly would the vet do?" Hank asked.

"He would probably make an incision about six or eight inches long, then go in there and take the fat out, you know using liposuction, then sew him back up. Nothing to it really."

Chapter 11

———

JERRY STEVENS LED MAGIC out of his stall and down to a fenced pasture the approximate size of most show rings. The Albuquerque National Arabian Horse Show was coming up at the end of October, less than three months away. Stevens felt in his bones that Black Magic had a good chance to place in the top three, if not win, especially after all the buzz from his Region XII victory. But, he wanted to be sure the stallion was ready to spin the judges' heads into a knot with his beauty and showmanship.

Walking through the grass with his horse, Jerry called Linda on his cell.

"Hey, Linda, I've been thinking about my expansion plans and the breeding service. We were interrupted the other day. You were suggesting the quantity of straws to ship."

"That stallion of yours is very virile. When you really start shipping his semen, I think you can cut back on the number of straws of frozen semen. Begin with eight straws, and, if they take the way I think they will, we'll drop it to four. After all, we can always send more if the owner doesn't have success with his mare."

"Sounds good, Linda. If Magic does as well as I believe he can at the Albuquerque show, he should really be in demand for breeding."

"In which case, you can charge the same, because after all, he will be even more valuable."

"Thanks. I'll update the figures on my spreadsheet. Talk to you later."

"Jerry," Barbara called out to her husband as she jogged toward the pasture. "Did you move Desiree from the south pasture?"

Looking up, Jerry saw his wife running through the grass to the wood-railed fence. "No. Why?"

Gripping the top beam, Barbara climbed up on the bottom rail, her brows drawn together, eyes darting in all directions. Black Magic now at the fence nuzzled her outstretched hand.

"Tony just texted me. He went over to check on her and she's not there. Hang-on, let me get my cell—it's Tony."

Jerry watched his wife, her phone to her ear, listening intently to Tony, the farm's manager. She suddenly looked up at her husband, fresh alarm spreading across her face. "Jerry and I will be right down. Stay where you are."

"What's the matter?" From her scrunched up face he knew something was wrong.

"The fence was cut. Desiree is nowhere to be seen. She's gone. Oh, Jerry, who would take her?"

"I don't know. Let me put Magic back in his stall. I'll get the tractor and pick you up." Jerry ran to the pasture's gate, Black Magic trotting beside him.

Barbara jumped off the fence and ran to the gate to help her husband swing it open. "You go on, I'll close the gate. Meet you up by the barn."

"How far along is Desiree?" Jerry yelled back over his shoulder.

"Six months." Barbara flipped the iron latch shut on the post and ran up towards the tractor.

Having secured Black Magic in his stall, Jerry quickly jogged to the tractor, gave Barbara a hand up, and turned the key. The noisy engine sprang to life. Bumping along over the ruts in the pastures, Barbara jumping out to open gates, then closing them after the tractor sped through, they finally caught sight of Tony. They drove up to him, standing with hands on his hips. Jerry immediately saw where the fence had been cut. Whoever had done it had pulled the wire fencing open to allow the mare through and then stretched it back in place. From a distance a person would not see the intrusion.

"Tony, order that chain-link fence. I knew I should have done it before now." Jerry looked to the other side of the fence. "Where could she be?" he muttered to himself. Digging his cell out, he punched Linda's code.

"Hi, it's me again. Desiree is missing."

"What do you mean missing?"

"We think she's been stolen. If she's given feed and water, and not treated badly, is she likely to be okay?"

Barbara plunked down on the grass—staring at the breach in the fence.

"She should be fine," Linda said. "But who would steal her?"

"That's what Barbara and I are asking ourselves. I can't believe she's gone. Whoever has her had better not hurt her ... she's six months along ... with Magic's foal ... how could this happen?" Jerry removed his cap, rubbed the top of his shaved head, then wiped the sweat from his face with his arm. Holding the phone to his ear, cap in his other hand, he stared down at the ground slowly shaking his head.

"Have you called the police? That David Milhous seemed sharp. I'm expecting him here today to question Rick Thurmond's parents."

"Thanks for the suggestion." Jerry snapped his cell shut and climbed on the tractor. "Come on, hon, let's go back to the house. Linda suggested I call the police detective who's working her intern's case."

Barbara grabbed Jerry's outstretched hand and swung up on the tractor. She saw that look in her husband's eyes—worry, anxiety, and fear of harm coming to Desiree. She knew Jerry was going to head to the kitchen to cook—his way of coping with his fears. A vegan with a passion for mixing up his own recipes, but only when he was under stress, had proved to be a boon for friends and neighbors. He didn't just prepare dinner for two, but usually enough to feed the entire county. Depending on how many days he stayed in the kitchen was in direct relationship to the time Barbara spent delivering his delicacies.

This time was going to be especially stressful.

———

THE FEED TRUCK DRIVER barreled down the road. Answering the ring of his cell phone, driving with the other hand and watching the curves in the road, the caller began screaming at him.

"I just got your message from last night, you dumb bastard. What do you mean you stole a mare from Steven's farm? How stupid can you get?"

"Hold on. That mare is worth a lot of money. She happens to be pregnant."

"So what."

"So what? I'll tell you so what. Black Magic is the daddy. So maybe I couldn't get a hold of his semen, but now we'll have a foal with his DNA. We'll start there."

Chapter 12

———

LINDA CRANKED UP THE AC in the conference room. She had shown the Thurmonds the examination room where their son had died and they were now meeting with the police. Mrs. Thurmond was mopping tears from her eyes with a tissue as her husband tried, unsuccessfully, to console her. Tension was as high as the humidity in the small room.

Detective Milhous paused his questioning to give Mrs. Thurmond time to compose herself. The couple had waited until Sunday to travel south from Atlanta to Ocala. They hoped an extra couple of days would help them cope with the sudden death of their son, but the wait only turned out to heighten their distress. They could not come to grips with the fact he was taken from them.

"How about some iced tea?" Linda said in a soft voice as she tried to alleviate the tension.

"Sounds like a good idea," David said.

The Thurmond's nodded in agreement.

"Let me help you, Dr. Turner." David followed Linda out of the room.

"I made some tea this morning. I was afraid this was going to be an emotional meeting. It's turning out even worse than I thought." Entering the lab, Linda pulled out a pitcher of tea from the refrigerator. Glasses were already on a tray along with the sugar bowl. "I'll put these ice cubes right in the pitcher. Hope nobody wants lemon. David, if you'll carry the tea and these napkins, I'll get the tray. Aren't you hot in that uniform? I'd be sweating up a storm." She chuckled in spite of the solemn occasion.

"It does get a bit sweaty at times," he replied.

"By the way, did you get a call from Jerry Stevens about his mare being stolen?"

"Yes. I told him I'd come over this afternoon. Here, let me hold the door for you."

Back in the conference room, Linda served the tea. Mrs. Thurmond had stopped crying and looked expectantly at the detective.

Mr. Thurmond spoke up. "Detective, when can we see Richard, and when do you think we can make arrangements to have him transported back to Atlanta? We have to get on with the funeral arrangements."

"I talked with the medical examiner and he said you could come by the morgue anytime tomorrow. He'll be able to give you a good idea as to when he'll release the body. He's doing another battery of tests and, of course, he's hoping the autopsy will reveal some answers. Both you and Linda say he didn't have a drug problem yet cocaine was found in his blood. There seems to be many unanswered questions. I'm hoping that the ME can clear a few of them up. His death is becoming more and more suspicious."

"What are you saying, Detective?" Mrs. Thurmond leaned forward, a fresh flow of tears cascading down her cheeks. "Are you telling us there may have been foul play or a bad accident or—"

Mr. Thurmond cut in. "Are you saying our son could have been murdered?"

"Let's not jump to conclusions. Wait to see what the ME has to report. Here, I've written down the directions to the morgue. When you get there, ask for Dr. Alex Grant. He's the ME." David handed the piece of paper to Mr. Thurmond.

"I have to be going now, Dr. Turner. I'll call you as soon as I get Dr. Grant's report." David left the room closing the door behind him. He stepped out the front entrance into a blast of hot air.

"Whoa, excuse me, officer. Hey, hold on a minute, I almost didn't recognize you in your uniform, David. It is you isn't it with all that hardware around your waist?"

"Well, Liz, fancy meeting you here, and I see our dogs are behaving themselves."

"I did recognize Whiskey, but, of course, I didn't know you were a police officer."

"Do you have a horse here?" David asked.

"No, I just dropped by to see Linda. Do you have a horse here?"

"No, I came to see the Turners. I'm sure you heard about the death of their young intern."

"Oh, yes ... I did ... on the news. Bye. See you out on the road."

Chapter 13

ANOTHER STICKY DAY IN PARADISE, Liz thought, filling Maggie's water bowl. "I won't be long, girl. We missed our run the last two days, so how about you and I go to the dog park after dinner. Take care of the office while I'm out." Maggie seemed to sense she wasn't going with her mistress and didn't look up from her prone position on her pillow. She did manage one thump of her tail. Fifteen minutes later Liz pulled into the morgue's parking lot. Linda told her yesterday that the ME would have the final results today as to what caused the intern's death.

Walking along the gray, cement-block corridor to the ME's office the familiar odor of bleach permeated the air. Opening the door to his office, she was hit again with the even stronger stench of disinfectant. Dr. Grant, hearing the bell trip from his lab, scooted into his office expecting to find Detective Milhous.

"Hello, miss. Are you lost?"

"I'm looking for the medical examiner."

"Well, you found him."

"Oh, hello," Liz said with a smile. "My name is Elizabeth Stitchway."

"How do you do, Elizabeth Stitchway. I'm Dr. Grant, Alex Grant." The two shook hands and Dr. Grant nodded to the chair facing his desk for Liz as he sat down rubbing his back. "Darned if this back isn't kicking up on me again. One of my helpers is out sick so I'm having to do most of the testing. Tell me, what can I do for you?"

"Here, let me give you my business card," Liz said retrieving one of her cards from her tote.

"My, your own business ... private investigator?"

"Absolutely, and that's why I'm here. The owner of the Turner Equine Reproduction Center asked me to see if you had determined her intern's cause of death. She said Detective Milhous indicated you might have the results today. Dr. Turner said you found cocaine in his blood, but that you also thought there was more to it."

"Well, Miss Stitchway, it's a sad case I'm afraid. So young. Detective Milhous called. He's on his way here to discuss my findings. The Thurmonds were over earlier to identify the body and I expect them back later today with the arrangements to have their son transported to Atlanta for burial.

Alex opened a manila file folder on his desk. Picking up the top sheet, he scanned the page looking over the top of his horn-rimmed glasses. He was interrupted when the door to the lab opened and a middle-aged man in green scrubs poked his head in.

"Dr. Grant, can you come here a minute? I don't know where you want me to put the blood samples we took this morning."

"Certainly. I'll be right with you." Grant laid the document he was holding down on the folder. "Excuse me a minute, Miss Stitchway. I'll be right back."

Liz nodded that she'd wait. She stood and walked around the room, then casually stepped behind the ME's desk, taking a quick peek at the sheet he had been looking at. The first sentence, bold type, underlined, jumped out at her: "Richard Thurmond–cause of death cardiac arrest brought on by a large dose of cocaine followed by a taser shot at close range."

She scooted back to the front of the desk and sat down, her mind processing the information she had just read. If Rick was tased, that could explain the exam room being in such a disarray. He would have convulsed, a seizure, knocking things around unable to stop himself, and ending up in a fetal position.

Dr. Grant returned from his lab along with a draft of refrigerated air. "Let's see, where were we?" The ME sat down at his desk and closed the file. "Oh, yes, the intern. I'm sorry, my dear, but I'll have to let Dr. Turner or the police fill you in on what I found."

The door suddenly opened and Detective Milhous in full uniform, his large biceps resulting from a free-weight regimen causing his shirtsleeves to bulge, filled the room with his presence. He stopped short when he saw Liz.

"Liz, fancy seeing you here." Looking at Dr. Grant, David's eyes opened wide and a slight nod of his head as if asking, what's she doing here?

"Hello, Detective … Detective David Milhous," Liz said sticking her hand out and grinning.

David gave her hand a pump. "It seems I'm the only one in the dark here. You're Liz … Liz who?"

"Oh, I thought you two had met. David, this is Elizabeth Stitchway. She's a private investigator."

"Ah, a PI. Well, that explains a few things."

"I have to be running along," Liz said. "Nice talking with you, Dr. Grant, and you, too, Detective."

"My pleasure, Miss ... it is Miss?" David asked.

"Yes. Miss Stitchway." Liz flashed a megawatt smile his way.

"Miss Stitchway. Maybe we'll run into each other again sometime."

"You never can tell, Detective. Maybe we will."

Chapter 14

———

KUWAITI PRINCE SULTAN AL AMRI preened in front of the mirror in his stateroom. He had enjoyed the journey in his yacht to Monaco. Three beautiful young women, a blonde, and two brunettes had catered to his every need. Now that he was moored out in the bay, he was anxious to get to the purpose of his trip. Gambling. But not just any gambling—he wanted to double his fortune in the coming days.

His fortune wasn't small but nor was it enough to properly build the House of Al Amri, a farm with stables filled with the finest Arabian horses in the world—for show, for racing, and for breeding. He foresaw the day when breeders around the world would seek his stallions out to improve the bloodlines of their foals. He had just finalized the purchase of a multi-million dollar property and now he needed the funds for phase two—building the stables and stocking them with beautiful Arabian horses.

Tonight he would not wear his robes, or the white silk headdress with the Agal, a thick, double-black cord that held the scarf in place. No, tonight he chose a black Botegga Veneta suit, white satin shirt, and a black silk tie. The shirt's French cuffs were held in place by gold cufflinks studded with two-carat diamonds. His six-foot-two muscular frame was topped with short, stylishly cut black hair, and a full black moustache adorned his upper lip. His mind wandered from the man in the mirror to his plans for the evening and on to the nights to come during his stay in Monaco.

Millions of dollars were known to change hands on any given night in the principality's casinos and Sultan's goal was to be the recipient of such winnings. He had visited Monaco many times to observe the winners, and, more important, the losers, and how both groups handled themselves. There was a pattern to how the stakes grew larger and larger as the evening progressed and the players, consuming more alcohol, became careless with their wagers, be it poker, craps, blackjack or some other exotic table game. He had already made arrangements with his crew as to when he would depart his yacht, and where and what time he was to be picked up to return from his night's work. At the soft knock on his door, he turned away from the mirror ready to begin his evening at the tables.

Sultan's driver wound his way up the narrow, serpentine road to the casino. The prince climbed out of the car and his driver left to return to the bottom of the hillside—parking at the casino was not allowed. Sultan entered the Casino de Monte-Carlo a little after nine o'clock. The Monte Carlo was the grandest of all the casinos. It was legendary and thought to be the most prestigious in all of Europe. The women wore their finest gowns and most glittering diamond earrings and necklaces which set off shards of light under the many crystal chandeliers. The men were debonair in their suits and ties, some choosing tuxedos. Of course, there were those whose dress was more casual, but Sultan had learned not to be fooled by what the players wore. People of means didn't always flash that fact about with fancy clothes.

The prince wagered at a roulette table to start his blood flowing for the bigger games, games where the mind had to be clear and sharp. He would soon move on to the Sun Casino where the pots at the poker tables drew the crowds—and the money. He planned to enjoy himself the first night. He had already spotted the big players and knew when they would start their evening's entertainment. He also wanted to identify the high rollers, especially the reckless ones. Gambling began to get rolling after ten o'clock and was at the most intense after midnight. By the time he returned to his yacht he had added several thousand dollars to his account. An appetizer.

He stayed on the yacht during the day. When he was younger he would visit the perfume factory, buying vials of the intoxicating mixtures as gifts for some of the more attentive bare-breasted women he encountered on the beach, or at the hotel's swimming pool where he had reserved a room when he needed to refresh himself. From the profusion of flowers native to the area, their scents captured in the pretty perfume bottles were always appreciated by the beautiful ladies.

The days wore on and Sultan finally felt he was ready to make his move, to go for the big strike. He had eliminated the players who dropped out because the pots were too rich for them and narrowed his sights to those who seemed to bet with abandon.

His last night started well. He went all-in several times and was well on his way to amassing his goal, increasing his stake with every hand. He felt good. Very good indeed. It didn't matter if he lost a hand here and there, or the times he should have folded but hung in for one more card certain it would be the exact one he needed. But he began to lose count of the bad hands—still winning a few pots now and then. Sultan didn't notice that his losing hands seemed to spur on his opponents as they waited to go in for the kill.

Sultan suddenly realized that his chips were dwindling. He urged himself to buckle down. He became tense. He could feel his armpits grow damp, his breathing became shallow and fast. Then the unthinkable miracle happened—he was dealt a straight flush. He glanced at the faces of his opponents, trying to read their expressions. They showed no sign of holding a winning hand that could beat him. *Someone would have to have a royal flush for God sake.* This hand would change his luck. He slowly pushed his chips into the pile. He was all in.

The players threw up their hands, stood up, and left the table grumbling that it was too rich for them. All that is but one. The one player who didn't budge from his chair, an American cattleman, matched Sultan's chips. "Whatcha got?" the cattleman asked.

"Ah, well let's see," Sultan said as he slowly laid his cards down—the 5, 6, 7, 8, and 9 of hearts. Sultan, a smile crossing his face, looked up at the cattleman.

The rancher looked at Sultan, his face sullen, and then a twinkle appeared in his eyes, lips drawing up into a slow grin.

"Sorry, partner, but I have this here Royal Flush." The man laid down the ten, jack, queen, king, and ace of spades.

Chapter 15

―――

SEPTEMBER BROUGHT AN END to the monsoon season in Arizona, and the residents of Black Canyon City heaved a sigh of relief. However, the new month did usher in a few dust storms raising tempers periodically. Rusty never paid attention to the weather unless it impacted her grooming, or the schooling of the horses on her ranch.

She had befriended a new veterinarian, Victor Bennett. A vet who saw things her way, and who was an artist when it came to performing surgery on the horses, enhancing their beauty and upping their potential to win in the show ring. At least that's how Rusty and Victor felt about the matter of equine cosmetic surgery when she discussed potential operations with him.

Today Victor was showing Rusty his latest handiwork with the throatlatch operation on Sampson, the Peterson's stallion. It had been just under a week since they transported Sampson and the yearling filly, Sunny, to Burns Arabian Horse Ranch.

Rusty ran her hand down the handsome stallion's withers and then down the side of his neck. Victor lifted Sampson's head to show her the incision which was only visible on either side of the large bandage. She had seen the seven-inch cut earlier, under the horse's jowl, where Victor sucked out the fat. There were two holes on each side, with tubes extending out, draining the fluid to keep the swelling down. Now the stallion had a bandage taped around his ears and underneath his jowl to hold the dressing in place.

Victor stroked Sampson's nose as he talked to Rusty. "When we take the bandages off, I'll give you some ointment to put on the incision to help it heal and to promote hair growth. Pretty soon you won't see a mark where I took out the fat."

"He's going to be terrific. I can't wait to parade him in the ring," Rusty said.

"Don't try to school him too soon. I performed the same operation on a mare down in Tucson. The owner got antsy and prematurely started schooling her even though I had warned him to wait until the incision had healed completely. He didn't listen and a couple of areas split open from the horse stretching when he posed her. He told me later that a local vet came and stitched up the cut."

"Did you stick him with the same $5000 fee you charged me?" she asked grinning.

"Actually, a little more. You get a special rate," he said smiling back at her. Victor picked up his medical bag leaning against the outside of the stall. "I put together some of the ointment I mentioned and bandages for you. If you need more, you know where to reach me."

"Thanks, Victor. You are a true artist," Rusty said smiling up at him. She stood back to look how improved the horse's neckline was going to be—once the swelling went down. She was so pleased with the results she leaned in and gave Victor a big hug. He held her a little too long to her liking and she quickly backed away from his embrace. *I won't let that happen again,* she thought. "Have to run. See you later." She turned, jogged out of the barn, mounted her horse, Black Panther, and galloped up to the house.

———

RUSTY STOPPED IN THE KITCHEN for a large glass of iced tea, poked a lemon wedge into the glass and headed for her office. Firing up her computer, she leaned back enjoying the cold beverage. Glancing out the window she saw Victor's truck pulling out onto the highway.

Logging into her email account, she glanced through her messages, deleting most, filing a few, and leaving some to be dealt with later. At the bottom of the list, hitting her inbox sometime during the night, was a message from a Prince Sultan Al Amri. Subject: My October Visit to Albuquerque.

Clicking the message, the full text displayed on her screen. She couldn't believe her good fortune. She read the message again, stood up, paced around the fourteen-foot, red-oriental carpet, looked at the bookcases lining two walls, then out the picture window facing the barn—it was all a blur. Sitting down at her desk, she read the message again, then hit the print button. The printer spit out the one-page message. Rusty grabbed it and ran from the room, squealing for her father.

"Dad, Dad, where are you?"

"Here, in the living room. What's got my little firecracker so wound up?" he asked laughing at his daughter's antics as she twirled in front of him waving a piece of paper.

Rusty planted her feet, threw her head back, eyes closed, and inhaled deeply. At the count of three, her green eyes flew open and she pushed the printed sheet into her father's chest. "Read. Read this."

"Have you heard of this prince before?" Charles asked as he continued to read.

"No, but you can bet those Justin boots you have on I'm going to know more about him than his mother does before the October show."

"Says here he's looking to improve his Arabian stock. My, my. Wants a champion stallion and three mares, all must have placed in the top three of a national competition. He does say, 'money is always a consideration.'"

"Do you know what this means, Dad? It means Burns Arabian Horse Ranch will be on the map. My goal to attract clients from around the world will be possible when I include on the website that this prince person is ecstatic with his horses and my service. That's what it means, Dad."

"Well, yes, I see. But first you have to come up with the horses, the ones he wants, ones that he sees with his own eyes that you, Burns' Arabians, are the one to buy from."

"How lucky is this? I have the perfect stallion in the barn, the Peterson's Arabian. He's a champion or will be once I show him in Albuquerque. I'll begin schooling him for the show soon. He's already placed third, no reason why he can't move up to champion or reserve. Now I have to scout around for the mares—a couple comes to mind. Gotta run, Dad. I have work to do." She threw her arms around her father, planted a kiss on his cheek, and ran back to her office.

———

YUMA DIDN'T KNOW HOW to handle the dilemma facing him. He sat on a hay bale in the barn, chewing a piece of hay, head down. Sampson whinnied in the stall behind him.

"I hear you big fella." Yuma took off his worn brown cowboy hat running his gnarled fingers over the felt. Bowing his head, he muttered to himself, "Ain't right, cutting an animal ... for no good reason. No, sir. Ain't right." He rubbed his shoulder and jammed his hat back on his head. He stood up and slowly looked back at Sampson. He spit on the floor, hitched his jeans up, and walked out of the barn. His stride quickened over the desert sand and then on the fieldstone path that led to the house.

Yuma was almost a part of the Burns family and had full access to their home. Even so, he was respectful and always rang the distinctive chime on the back door before entering, letting them know he was there.

Hearing the doorbell, Charles sauntered into the kitchen. "Yuma, how're you doing today? Or should I ask, how're we doing?" Charles extended his hand in greeting.

"That's why I'm here, Mr. Burns." After all the years he had worked for the family he still could not bring himself to call the mister and misses by their first names. Rusty was different—he had cared for her since she was baby.

Charles noticed the leathered face of the older man was set in a grim expression. "Something bothering you, Yuma? You know you can count on me to help with whatever it is."

"Yes, sir, I know and I'm banking on that. But I just don't know if it's my place to talk to you, but I've got to talk to someone."

"Come on, man. What is it?"

"Well, it's about Rusty, the new vet, and that stallion, Sampson."

"Yes, yes, go on."

Yuma squared his shoulders, looked Charles in the eyes, and plunged on. "They cut that horse. The vet Victor performed surgery on Sampson. To their way of thinking, to fix his throat to be sleek. Took out some fatty tissue and sewed him back up. They asked me to apply hot packs on the wound several times a day. Now he has a big bandage and I'm to change that until the stitches dissolve. It ain't right, Mr. Burns. Rusty is going to start refreshing his training, more schooling, for the Albuquerque show."

"Did you talk to Rusty about your concerns?"

"Yes. She just laughed it off, said I was a crazy old Indian—my concern for animals and all. Said that it was just a little cosmetic surgery."

Chapter 16

GUNNING HER PICKUP TRUCK down the highway, Rusty's thoughts were not on her driving but on which of her clients' Arabs she should pick to show to Sultan. She was on her way to Victor's clinic to get his opinion. For some reason she had pulled on one of her favorite pair of tooled reddish-leather boots, her new stretch jeans cinched in with a leather belt studded with silver. She topped off the outfit with a white silk, sleeveless blouse with a deep V-neck. The outfit definitely revealed her curves, which was her aim. She was beginning to change her mind about the handsome vet and could see it might be useful if they had a closer relationship.

Pulling into his clinic she was happy to see the parking lot was empty. Climbing out of her truck, she slung her bag over her shoulder and walked briskly to the front entrance. Victor was talking with his receptionist and did a double-take when Rusty walked in.

"Well, hello. You didn't tell me you were coming over."

"Do you have time to chat?" Rusty asked, pleased with his reaction at seeing her. "I need your advice."

"If I did have something scheduled, I would certainly cancel. Come on in my office."

Rusty smiled at the receptionist, who had a slight frown on her face, and followed Victor. She took a seat facing his desk as he closed the door behind them.

"So what advice could the inimitable Rusty Burns want from me. I trust Sampson is healing okay."

"Beautifully, in fact." Rusty pulled a piece of paper from her shoulder bag and handed it to Victor. "Just read this and you'll see why I'm excited."

Victor took the paper from her hand but had a hard time pulling his eyes away from her. After his eyes drifted from her eyes and slowly down her curves, he turned to the typed sheet. "Sultan?"

"A prince from Kuwait. Go on, read it."

"Whoa, this will put a fine feather in that cowgirl hat you have on there. October. That gives you some time to pick the horses you want to show him."

"My thought exactly. Sampson will be the stallion I'll sell to him unless another one comes up. But I doubt another Arab will come along that could surpass him, especially now that he's perfect." Her full, red lips parted in a smile, green eyes sparkling above.

Victor lost his train of thought for a moment ... he was caught in her spell. She knew it and leaned a little closer over his desk. The silky V-neck fabric opened slightly following her movement.

"Yes ... yes, I agree, Sampson. Now, what about the mares?"

"I have two in mind ... here, take a look at their pictures." Rusty retrieved three photos from her bag. "The first two are regional champions. I'm working with them and I'll pick the best to show in Albuquerque. The third photo is a possibility, but I was hoping you might have some suggestions from the Arabs you've seen lately."

"As a matter of fact, I do. I know a beauty. Twice the judges said she could be a champion but disqualified her because of a flaw. It's a darn shame, too, because she's breathtaking. Beautiful body." Victor's eyes once again took in the vivacious woman who sat in front of him.

"What's the matter with her?"

"She has white sclera—in both eyes."

"The eyeball?"

"Yes. I've treated this for a couple of owners who wanted to improve their horses. You put ink in the sclera, filling it in."

"I've heard about that," Rusty said. "It's known as tattooing isn't it?"

"That's right, and the procedure requires quite extensive aftercare."

"Like what?" Rusty leaned back in her chair, thoughts running through her head, wondering if she could get away with showing such a horse to Sultan.

"The horse has to stay out of the light—closing all the barn doors, keeping it as dark as possible. The eyes swell and you have to put ointment in each eye three times a day. Of course, you won't be alone. I'll come out every day to check on how they're healing."

"How much do you charge for this procedure, Victor?"

"$1200. A bargain really. The results are dramatic."

"Do you think it's cheating?"

"Rusty, people do cosmetic surgery all the time. I'm just perfecting the horse's image."

"How long does this aftercare take before I could show her?"

"A month or six weeks ... not long, especially if she heals quickly."

"What are the chances she'd pass the genes on to her foals?"

"It could happen, but it's much more likely if the sire has the genes, far less likely if it's the dam. I also know of another mare. She was a reserve champion at nationals last year."

Rusty ambled over to the window in his office which overlooked the parking lot. Victor had her mind spinning with possibilities.

"Sometimes, the ears just don't look right." Victor watched Rusty as she stood with her back to him.

"Pardon me. Ears?" She said turning to face him.

"Yea, I can do some reshaping, trimming."

"I have to think about this. When can I see the mare you were talking about?" Rusty's eyes fixed on Victor.

"Well, that depends."

"On what?"

"If you'll have dinner with me tomorrow night."

"Victor, are you bribing me?"

"Maybe. I know this terrific ranch that serves the best barbequed steaks in Arizona, along with a country-western band that will have your toes tapping."

"Well, mister, okay, but only if I can see the mare in the morning."

"If I show you the mare, you won't weasel out of dinner will you?"

"That's for me to know and you to find out. But you had me with the country-western band."

Chapter 17

———

IT WAS MID-SEPTEMBER and Floridians breathed a little easier but remained on guard. No one dared mention the "H" word. They had been spared so far—no hurricanes this season. Jerry Stevens and his financial advisor Joe Rocket, dressed casually in jeans and T-shirts, had finished lunch. Joe, looking over Jerry's shoulder at the computer screen, was now explaining the Excel spreadsheet he had prepared for Stevens' proposed expansion.

Sitting down in the chair beside Jerry's desk, Joe looked at his client who had shut down his computer. "Well, what do you think of the numbers I came up with for your project?"

"They look good, Joe. Do you think I'll have any trouble borrowing the first hundred thousand from the bank?" Jerry asked. He hit the button on his CD player, and the room was instantly filled with the soft sounds of country music. Flipping on the intercom, he said, "Barbara, can you bring in a couple of beers and bring one for yourself. I'd like you to join us."

Her voice came through the speaker. "Love to. I'll be with you in a second."

"With your credit, I think they'll cough it up on your signature alone. They know how valuable your land is even without the Arabs," Joe said, steepling his fingers together.

The door to the study opened and Jerry jumped up to help his wife. She put a tray holding three bottles of beer, a bowl of pretzels, and Jerry's hummus dip on the coffee table. They each picked up a beer, unscrewed the caps, and clinked the bottles together.

"Cheers. Here's to a successful expansion of Stevens Arabian Horse Farm," Joe said.

"We'll drink to that won't we, honey," Jerry said smiling at Barbara.

"How do the numbers look, Jerry?" Barbara asked.

"Actually, they look good. I'll take the proposal Joe put together to our banker tomorrow. Get a read on what he thinks. If he gives us the go ahead, I'm going to call a vet in Jacksonville who was recommended by another breeder, a neighbor. I'm feeling a little vulnerable storing all of Magic's frozen semen at Linda's center." Taking a bite of pretzel, he turned to Joe. "The insurance company contacted me the other day to go over the renewal. When we went through the policy they said they couldn't cover the frozen semen any longer unless I stored it at more than one facility." Jerry took another swallow of beer.

"Now that we have an idea on the value, and my goodness the potential value if all goes well at the show in Albuquerque, we have to up the coverage," Barbara said. "By the way, Joe, did Jerry tell you we had a mare stolen? She's carrying Magic's foal."

"Jerry, you didn't tell me about a horse being stolen. How … when did this happen?" Joe said sitting forward in his chair.

"Someone cut the fence, and I guess she walked out free as you please, several weeks ago now," Jerry said. "I called the police and a detective dropped by, looked at the fence and the ground on both sides, but she hasn't turned up yet. Barbara and I are sick about it. Probably why I didn't tell you before … we can't bring ourselves to believe she's not still out in the pasture. Linda Turner, our vet, sent out an email—she has a list of all the veterinarians in central Florida, plus a few north and south—asking them to be on the lookout for Desiree. We called all of our friends to be sure they kept their eyes open for her. Nothing. It's like she never existed." Jerry ran his hand over his shaved head and slumped back in his chair.

"Does she have your brand on her somewhere?" Joe asked.

"We don't brand Arabs anymore. However, all registered purebreds are DNA Typed."

"I don't know if you ever saw her, Joe," Barbara said. "Desiree is a beautiful lady. Took Reserve National Champion in Oklahoma a few years back."

"What's a reserve champion?"

"Reserve is second to the champion." Jerry said, pulling himself up straight.

"Uh, I'd say she's pretty valuable then especially carrying the foal. I hope she turns up soon. I would think it likely a vet might spot her."

"That's what we're hoping, but no luck so far," Jerry said. Standing up, he walked to the window and looked out over the pastures.

"Is that why I received three loaves of raisin bread?" Joe asked with a half smile.

"You got it," Barbara replied. "The days after Desiree went missing our kitchen looked like a national bake-off."

"I have a friend," Joe said. "Actually I saved her life in a hurricane a few days after I was released from prison, out on good behavior I might add."

"Yes, we know your story," Jerry said with a grin, returning to his chair. "But what's this about a girl?"

"Her mail truck was blown into a canal. She almost drowned. But anyway, she turned around and worked on my case when nobody else believed I was framed. She was instrumental in my getting the verdict reversed. She's now a private investigator. Her business is new so she might have more time to spend on finding your mare than the police."

"What's her name, and does she cover this area?" Barbara asked.

"She opened an office in Ocala, downtown near the city square. Her name is Elizabeth Stitchway. Hang on, I'm sure I have her new number on my cell ... here it is." Joe wrote Liz's number on a piece of paper and handed it to Barbara.

Observing the Stevens and the obvious love they shared for each other, Joe suddenly had to see Liz. Now he had a good excuse to call her—a lead for a new client.

Chapter 18

LUCKILY THE THUNDERSTORM had passed on to the east coast. Liz tossed her umbrella on the floor and stepped out of her car. The last time she met a man in a bar was two years ago. Now she was meeting the same man and her heart fluttered at the thought of seeing Joe again. He had surprised her when he called earlier in the day with an invitation to meet him for drinks at Harry's, facing Ocala's city square.

Entering the restaurant, her eyes took a moment to adjust to the dimly lit bar.

"Can I show you to the dining room?" the hostess asked picking up a menu.

"No ... I'm meeting a friend." Liz looked around the corner into the bar. "I see him, thanks anyway."

Joe saw her walking toward the table and stood up to greet her. Taking her in his arms with a warm embrace, he leaned back a little looking into her soft brown eyes. He smiled, pulled her to him and slowly kissed her lips.

"God, it's good to see you, Stitch."

She smiled hearing the name only he called her. "Come sit down. I just got here, so I didn't order yet. What would you like?"

"Are you going to have a highball as usual?" Liz asked. *He looks wonderful,* she thought. *I've missed him.*

"Good memory. Yes, it's been a long day. Make it two," Joe said smiling up at the waitress. "And an order of Harry's Signature Crab Cakes and ... a plate of your VooDoo Shrimp." They both laughed remembering the same banter took place the last time they had drinks together. "Thanks, Christi," Joe said, handing the menus to the waitress, her name tag pinned to her black, short-sleeve blouse.

Joe turned back to Liz. "Stitch, you look beautiful. I like what you've done with your hair—it's softer around your face and a deeper color, almost auburn." Seeing her smile, he grasped her hand across the table. "Am I right?"

"I guess we both have a good memory. I'm glad you like it. How's business? I bet your old clients returned in droves after they heard you were back." Liz took her drink from Christi's hand with a quick smile.

"I don't know about droves, but enough were glad to hear from me when I called to say I was back in business. Of course, I threw in a few freebies to entice them to let me manage their investments again. I was meeting with one of them today, Jerry Stevens, when I thought of you."

"How's that?"

"He and his wife Barbara own the Stevens Arabian Horse Farm—"

"Oh, I've heard of them—here in Ocala."

"Just on the outskirts. Anyway, they had a prize mare stolen a little while ago. Stitch, you wouldn't believe how much money these Arabs sell for. Stevens told me that a stallion, a champion, went for five-point-five-million dollars. Breeding can be auctioned off at more than $5,000 for one stud fee. After Black Magic, he's Stevens' stallion, won a regional competition his stud fee went up over $3,000. Stevens had over two-hundred requests for information the first few days after the show."

"Wow! And you said one of his mares was stolen?"

"That's right. I saw your announcement in the paper that you opened your agency—congratulations by the way—and, well, I told him about you. You may get a call, or, you could also call him." Liz decided not to mention she was working for the equine center. One of her business rules was not to talk about one client in front of another client or friend—even if that friend was Joe.

"Thanks for the lead. I'll call him in the morning."

"Stitch, your dress ... as I remember you bowled me over when you wore it the last time—in a bar, sharing a drink. When you walked in just now ... why haven't we seen each other before this?"

"Joe, we've both been so busy. After your name was cleared—"

"Thanks to you." Joe took a sip of his drink and reached again across the table, but this time lifted it to his lips.

"Yes, well ... I quit the post office and went to work for Goodwurthy again, the detective agency, only now it was full time. He finally told me to leave, that he was kicking his little bird out of the nest. He said I was ready to start my own agency and he'd send clients to me when he couldn't handle their requests right away."

"Good man. I remember your talking about him."

"You said you saw my announcement, so you know it's only been a little over a month since I tacked up my shingle." Liz leaned back on the booth's wooden banquette. The flutters had disappeared.

"What?" Joe asked. "What's the matter?"

"Why haven't we seen each other? Today you called because you thought I might be able to help your client. It wasn't the thought of seeing me that made you call. And I ... I knew where you were. I've been following your comeback in the newspaper."

Joe leaned forward, laying his hand palm up on the table, inviting her hand in his. Liz didn't move. *It's too late,* she thought.

"Stitch, talk to me."

"I think we've run out of time, Joe. If we had wanted to see each other, to be with each other, to start a real relationship, we would have."

"What are you talking about? I want to see you. Lots."

"I think it's too late for you and me ... to be a couple. We're both wrapped up in our fledgling businesses. We have new lives. We're in different places than we were two years ago. You were vulnerable, just getting out of prison. I was stuck as a mail carrier. Now look at us. Joe, I'm not saying we won't ever be a couple, but it just doesn't work for us now."

"Maybe ... I guess you're right. Here, give me your hand."

Liz leaned forward slightly and put her hand in his, her face showing the pain of ending something, maybe for good.

"We can at least be friends, can't we?" Joe said.

"Oh, yes, and we don't have to wait for two years to have another drink together." She squeezed his hand, a faint smile crossing her lips.

Chapter 19

———

THE NEXT MORNING Liz and Maggie were climbing the backstairs to her office when she heard her phone ringing. Scampering up the last few steps, fumbling with her key ring, she finally pushed the door open. She raced to pick up the receiver but the line was dead. She had missed the call and no message was recorded. Putting the receiver back in its cradle, she threw her shoulder bag on the client's chair and headed to the restroom sink to freshen Maggie's water.

"Wait a minute, you dimwit," she said to herself. "Some PI you are." Setting Maggie's water bowl in its usual spot she quickly walked back to her desk. Realizing her phone had the capability of storing the phone numbers of the callers, she hit the directory button and wrote down the last number. The caller ID displayed: Stevens Arabian Horse Farm.

"Look at that, Maggie, the people Joe told me about. Maybe we'll get some business." She selected the number and hit the connect button. A man answered identifying the farm.

"Hello, Mr. Stevens?"

"Yes."

"Sorry I missed your call. I was just opening my office door. Joe Rocket got in touch with me yesterday. He said you might call. What can I do for you?"

"I'm sure he told you about our stolen mare. Any chance you could come over?"

"I don't have anything scheduled right now," Liz said pumping her fist in the air. Maggie gave a soft bark joining in the excitement.

"That would be great. I'll give you directions to the farm and my wife and I will meet you outside the barn."

——

FOLLOWING STEVENS' DIRECTIONS down a winding rural road, Liz turned onto a gravel driveway to the barn. She saw a man sitting on a tractor talking to a woman resting on a bale of hay. Introductions followed along with handshakes and each asking to please address them by their first names. Jerry filled her in on the day Desiree disappeared.

"Barbara brought you a few copies of the flier we sent out. Linda Turner, the local equine vet, emailed the same flier to her contact list—most of them veterinarians."

So Linda is Stevens' vet, Liz thought. Small world. My first two clients not only know each other, but both are horse people and work closely together to boot. Liz took the color copies of the mare. "She sure is a beauty. It says here she's pregnant. I can't really tell from this picture."

"The picture was taken in May, her fourth month. She's now in her eighth month. A person who knows horses could tell she's pregnant, but a lay person might not," Barbara said.

"I'd like to see the pasture and the fence that was cut—"

"I thought you would," Jerry said. "That's why I asked you to meet us at the barn. Hope you don't mind riding on a tractor, but it's the easiest way to get down to the south pasture."

"No problem. It will remind me of the hay wagons my friends and I rode on a long time ago," Liz said smiling at the couple.

Jerry gave Liz a hand and she swung up perching on the large fender of the tractor's tire and waved goodbye to Barbara. They bumped along through the pastures until they reached the southern end of the farm and the repaired fence. Jerry turned to help Liz off the tractor but she had already jumped down and was inspecting the area.

"I see you replaced the fence. Where's the nearest road? Could someone drive a trailer up along the outside of your fence?" Liz asked, looking through to the field on the other side.

"Here is where the fence was cut. The nearest road is just over that ridge, so, yes, it's possible, but it would be easier to walk. The road's not far."

Liz retrieved a camera from her pants pocket and took a few pictures. "Can you tell me how to get to that road you mentioned? I'd like to take a look around."

"Sure. I'll draw you a map when we get back to the barn. It's rarely used. Sometimes people ask delivery drivers to use it to drop off loads of dirt or hay. There are a few neighbors who have horses, but not as extensive as our farm."

Jerry drove them back to the barn. "I hope you can find something, Liz. Both Barbara and I are feeling very uneasy. We can't bear the thought of never seeing Desiree again."

Liz jumped off the tractor as Jerry pulled a small notebook from his shirt pocket along with a pen, sketching out a map. Tearing the sheet from the pad, he handed the drawing to her.

"Here, I think you can find the road from this. The directions start at the end of our driveway." Jerry rubbed the top of his head. "After Desiree went missing, we had a call from our insurance company. A woman said they were going to cancel our coverage on the semen we store at the equine center. They said if we set up two storage facilities, they would continue the policy."

"So what are you going to do?"

"Just that. A neighbor suggested a vet up in Jacksonville who could store half of the straws, the other half remaining with Linda. He worked with this vet a little before moving here to Ocala."

"Excuse me, straws?"

"Sorry, a little horse jargon. After a collection of semen, we have a machine, a syringe like device, that transfers the fluid from the receptacle into individual straws and we either cool them or freeze them. A straw looks like a mini soda straw, but it's made of different material."

"Oh, I getcha."

"A straw contains one-half a cubic centimeter, cc, of semen. When a client negotiates a stud fee with a particular stallion, we ship them so many straws. Usually a fee includes four to eight so they have enough in case the first insemination doesn't develop into a pregnancy."

"Fascinating," Liz said. "Well, I'll be going, but I want to check out that utility road before I leave. Let me think over what happened and work up a few ideas on how we might pick up Desiree's trail. Please tell Barbara goodbye for me. It was a pleasure to meet you both. I'll get back to you soon."

———

FOLLOWING THE SKETCH Jerry had drawn on the paper, Liz stopped at where she thought was the edge of the pasture. She got out of her car to take a look around but realized she hadn't gone far enough. Driving another quarter mile or so, she again got out. Seeing a ridge ahead, which she surmised was the back of the one she'd seen from the other side, she walked the short distance to the top of the incline. Sure enough, there was Jerry's new fence. Glancing back at her car, and the terrain to where she was standing, she thought Jerry was right. Why risk getting hung-up with a trailer when you could walk it faster than driving. She continued to amble to the place in the fence that Jerry said they found the cut. She decided to return to her car taking a path that the thief may have walked with Desiree.

Keeping her head down and scanning the grassy ground from side to side with each step, she stopped short. To her left, about six inches, was a cigarette partially covered with dirt kicked up by the recent rain. Pulling a tissue from her shirt pocket, she carefully picked up the butt making sure she didn't touch it with her bare fingers. She continued walking to her car but didn't notice anything else unusual.

Chapter 20

———

"RISE AND SHINE. Rise and shine."

"What the?" David rolled out of bed, stood straight up, hands on hips, head tilted to one side.

Whiskey cocked her head, a guttural growl emanating from deep in her throat.

"Whiskey, my friend, it's that damn parrot we hauled home yesterday." David walked with long strides to the living room. "I knew we should have said no."

"Rise and shine. Rise and shine."

"I hear you, Polly. The least that girl could have done was name you something original," David said as he peeled away the night covering over the cage.

"Happy day. Happy day."

"Quite a vocabulary you have there, bird." David filled the feed container on the cage and added to the water. "Don't think I'm going to clean your house this morning. That little chore will have to wait."

"Happy day. Happy day."

David retreated to his bedroom and quickly pulled on his jogging gear. "Whiskey, I have a feeling this bird arrangement is not going to work out. Come on, let's go for our run." David snapped the leash on Whiskey and headed out to the road. He was hoping to see Liz this morning. It was obvious they were working the same cases and he didn't want her to get in his way. Of course, he was going to try to be diplomatic about it, but police work was police work, and he didn't want any interference from a girl PI.

He jogged at his usual pace for about a half a mile, looking back occasionally to see if Liz was in sight. He stopped as Whiskey suddenly stood her ground, twisting around on the leash. David turned and sure enough there were Liz and Maggie closing the distance between them.

"Hi, David, yes, you, too, Whiskey. How's everything this morning?" Liz asked, scratching the dog's ear.

The two humans and their dogs continued their jogging.

"In answer to your question, I had a rude awakening this morning," David said. "I couldn't interest you in a talking parrot could I?"

"Not on your life," Liz responded laughing. "Did you buy a bird?"

"No, I didn't. I guess I'm babysitting, but I fear the young woman may not come back. Another officer and I performed a drug raid, and this girl—she was an innocent bystander—shoved this cage in my arms, told me the bird food was in the closet, and she'd be back in two weeks to collect her."

They jogged on in silence. Finally David decided he might as well broach the subject he wanted to discuss with her. "I guess we're working the same cases."

"Oh, what are they?" Liz looked over at David and then back to the road.

"Come on, Liz, you know what I'm talking about."

"Well, just for conversation purposes, why don't you tell me anyway?"

"For starters, I bumped into you at the equine center after the kid was found dead. Unless I'm mistaken, Maggie is not a horse. And two, we saw each other at the morgue. I'm sure you talked to Linda about the taser, the cocaine and taser together causing him to die of cardiac arrest—so you probably figure, along with me, that Rick was murdered. Am I right?"

"Maybe. You said cases, like more than one. What else?"

"Linda Turner does a lot of work for Jerry Stevens."

"So."

"So, I'm sure she mentioned to you that one of his mares was stolen."

BLACK MAGIC | 83

"Maybe yes, maybe no. What are you getting at?" Liz stopped. Maggie suddenly feeling the leash tighten on her collar, trotted back to her mistress.

Damn, she's going to make this difficult, David thought. He and Whiskey put the brakes on, too. David turned to face Liz.

"This is police business and I don't want you compromising our efforts."

"Well, Detective, I'm a licensed private investigator. And if a client wants me to investigate something I'm going to investigate something."

"Look, don't get all huffy—"

"I'm not getting all huffy. And, for your information, I intend to continue working for my clients."

"Ah, caught you—clients. You are working for Stevens. Admit it."

"I admit nothing. Why don't you ask this Mr. Stevens."

"Truce," David said putting his hands in the air. He decided he'd better try a different approach. He took a deep breath, both dogs sitting on the asphalt looking up at him as he looked at Liz. She now had her hands on her hips, eyebrows raised, looking at him, waiting to hear what he came up with next.

"Why not work together?" David said. "Let me know if you come up with something and I'll let you know if we find something, unless, of course, I can't divulge the information." He hoped this would appease her.

"Sounds like a one-way flow of information—all in your direction. How about this—If I tell you something then you have to at least reciprocate, and I don't mean with something trivial. And, one more thing, and this is very important, or I say no deal."

"What's that?" Whiskey was tired of the new game and wanted to get going. She pulled on the leash, but David didn't budge.

"If I do come up with something, I'm the one who tells my client—not you. After all, if they've hired me, I have to produce or I don't get paid. On the other hand, if you find something first, then you tell them. I won't say anything. I won't comment until I know they know."

"You're talking in circles, lady, but I understand what you're saying. I agree."

"Deal?" Liz stuck out her hand.

"Okay, deal." David reluctantly took her hand, pumped it once, and then took up his jogging.

"You know," Liz said, keeping pace, "I think the murder and the stolen mare are connected."

"That's a stretch." *I wonder why she thinks that. Clues have gone cold for both cases, but it's an interesting idea,* David thought.

Liz glanced sideways at David. "You know, we could start this little exchange of information right now."

Keeping up the pace beside her but looking straight ahead, he said, "Yea? How so?"

"Well, I know you went to Rick Thurmond's mobile home he was renting. Did you check his computer, find any drugs or other interesting evidence?"

David mulled over what she had asked about. "Tell you what, let's turn around. How about a cup of coffee at my house? I don't like to run and talk so much. Maybe I can get you to take that parrot home with you."

"Yes, to the coffee," Liz said as they reversed directions, the dogs not missing a step with their masters' change in routine. "But, that other thing—not a chance."

———

"HAPPY DAY. HAPPY DAY."

"Is that all he can say?" Liz asked trying not to laugh as she sipped the piping hot coffee.

"Sure you don't want any half-and-half?" David asked giving his cup a generous shot.

Liz shook her head no.

"She said 'rise and shine' as soon as the sun came up this morning. It's too hot in here after we've been running. Let's move out to the deck."

"Too hot. Too hot."

They both laughed as they and the dogs vacated the house for the deck, shutting the door behind them.

"How do you know it's a she?" Liz asked.

"He, she … all I know is its name is Polly." The dogs immediately took off looking for squirrels.

"Okay, give. What did you find?"

"Nothing on the computer, but in the sink was paraphernalia for inhaling cocaine. So he was definitely into drugs. There was also a ground out cigarette butt."

"And, you told all this to Linda?" Liz asked.

"That's our deal—whoever finds something first, tells first."

"Well, she did tell me about the drug stuff, but she probably didn't think the cigarette was important. I, on the other hand, believing the two cases are connected, found what might be a piece of evidence to prove my theory when I saw Stevens a few days ago."

"Oh, and what did you find, and where did you find it, and when did you find it?" David asked in his best, deep prosecutorial voice.

"Very funny, Sherlock. I asked Mr. Stevens if there was a road anywhere near, you know, on the other side of the fence that was cut. After all, I doubt the thief rode Desiree off into the moonlight. There is a road, not very well maintained. I looked around with my Dr. Watson magnifying glass."

"And did Watson's glass spot anything?"

"Yes, it did. A cigarette butt."

"Liz, anybody could have thrown a butt down—it's been weeks."

"I know. I know. But seeing how you found a cigarette, I thought I'd reciprocate with a cigarette. I told Mr. Stevens about it, so our deal is in tack. You can pick it up at my office—you know, check it for matching DNA using the state's high-powered equipment."

Chapter 21

———

RUSTY AND VICTOR HAD become inseparable. She wasn't sure how it happened, but he was constantly by her side, from helping with the care of the Arabs, to picking her up at the end of the day to escort her to yet another lively, night spot for dinner.

Charles and Henry were happy for their daughter. They felt she worked too hard and wished she wasn't so consumed with the upcoming Arabian horse show. They were very worried about how she would react if the prince didn't buy the horses she had selected for him. It seemed to the Burns that Rusty was becoming overwhelmed by her expectations on the one hand, and her desire to complete the schooling of the numerous Arabs she planned to take to the show. They noticed the rising tension in her voice at the slightest setback. Owners were forever stopping at the ranch to witness the progress of their stallion or mare. They couldn't care less about Rusty's schedule. Their only concern was whether she was spending enough time with their animal. If, in their opinion, she was not, they told her so.

The Burns had discussed the possibility that their daughter might be headed for a nervous breakdown, a concern they would consider even more likely if they knew the tightrope Rusty was walking between what was sanctioned in preparing a horse for the ring and what was a disqualification—something ethically wrong or against her own moral standards.

However, Rusty tossed caution to the winds, after all Victor had only performed one surgery—a throat latch removing some fatty tissue. But then there was the tattooing of the eyes of one mare. He had a few more small surgeries scheduled—one on a mare, a fatty lump on her rump. "Just a little liposuction and she'll be perfect," Victor had explained. But then, there were the ears of the finest mare in the group which she planned to show to the prince. Victor suggested a little trim was needed.

Rusty fell into bed at night dreaming of being interviewed on television for receiving the top-trainer-of-the-year award, or an appearance on a show as the only dealer a potential buyer should see for the finest Arab stock.

The Burns hoped that Victor's presence would help to alleviate some of the stress their daughter was under, even if it was self-inflicted. They knew that Victor was taking Rusty to a swanky restaurant in Scottsdale for dinner this evening. Maybe an evening away from Black Canyon City would soothe Rusty's jangled nerves, for a few hours anyway.

───

A BOUQUET OF RED ROSES arrived in the afternoon. Rusty was about to pamper herself with a hot bath in her new Jacuzzi tub, when Theresa knocked on the door, handing her the bouquet that had just been delivered.

The water perfect, Rusty added a few drops of Jasmine bath oil. She placed the bouquet of roses on the edge of the marble tile that surrounded the tub. Removing the small card tucked into the bouquet, she read the hand-written note:

"To the most beautiful woman I've ever seen. I promise tonight will be special—one you will never forget. Victor."

Rusty smiled, holding the card to her cheek. She'd come to depend on Victor in so many ways. They had grown close and she didn't fight the attraction she had for him, pulling her to him. The first time he kissed her he sent her heart racing, taking her breath away. She found when she was with him at his clinic or her barn, or driving to see a horse, if their bodies touched, even a slight brush, electricity shot throughout her veins. When it was time to part for the day, there would always be an embrace, an embrace that was becoming more and more urgent.

Is this why I'm preparing myself for our evening tonight, for something special? She wondered. Last Saturday was wonderful, but he said goodnight at my doorstep. Is that why he sent me the roses and wrote the card to tell me tonight was going to be magical?

Letting her white silk robe slide slowly to the floor, she looked at her reflection in the mirrored wall. She saw her body in a different light. What would Victor think if he saw her like this? Would he see her like this tonight? If it was to be, she was ready. She had fantasized about what it would be like if he made love to her, stroked her skin. *Maybe tonight.*

Rusty stepped into the sweet-smelling water, laid her head back letting the jets warm her body. She closed her eyes. *Maybe tonight. Yes, it will be tonight.* She had never been with a man, never been touched by a man, never felt the desire to be held by a man. The men she had met were either too young or too old, leering at her as an object to be possessed, something they wanted to haul off to bed. But, of course, she had been too busy to give any of them the time of day ... until Victor. Everything changed after she met him. He understood her passion for the Arabs, for their beauty, for showing them to win the ultimate prize of a championship—the reward for perfection.

———

RUSTY PAUSED IN THE HALLWAY. She could hear her parents laughing with Victor, enjoying a cocktail together ... waiting for her. Well she would not disappoint him.

"Okay, what am I missing?" Rusty asked as she made her entrance.

The Burns looked up and stared at their daughter. They had never seen her as the woman who stood before them, a beautiful woman in a shapely black dress that clung to her curves, her flowing red hair cascading in soft waves over her shoulders and halfway down her bare back. Crystal earrings, her only jewelry, sent off shards of light. A single rose from Victor's bouquet was tucked behind her ear holding back her hair on one side. Stiletto black heels accentuated her firm calves, toned from hard work at the ranch.

"Rebecca!" Victor could say no more, moved by her beauty, but to call her by her given name. He stepped over to her, lifted her chin and kissed the crimson lips raised to his ... waiting.

"How about some of my special spicy buffalo wings," Theresa said, hustling into the expansive living room. "Oh, excuse me, I didn't mean to interrupt ... Miss Rusty, you look beautiful."

"You're not interrupting us at all, Theresa. Our daughter just threw us for a loop by wearing a dress. In fact, you came in at just the right time before I embarrassed her with how proud I am of her," Charles said.

Everyone chuckled, as Charles and Henry helped themselves to the wings. Victor mixed Rusty her favorite drink—an extra dry martini. Handing the drink to her, he softly touched the edge of her delicate, crystal glass with his, "To tonight," he whispered.

"To tonight." Rusty returned the toast, her eyes matching the sparkle of her earrings.

———

THE NIGHT PLAYED OUT exactly as Rusty had dreamed it would. The sun set behind the mountains to the west turning the desert into bright hues of gold and orange, then deep violet, and dark blue to black as it slipped out of sight. Torches lit the restaurant's patio around their table and tiny white lights adorned the trees and bushes.

Victor never moved from her side, holding her hand, or his arm around her waist, drawing her eyes to his. The music of violins drifted softly in the warm desert night air. They danced, swaying slowly along with a few other couples, but they didn't notice anyone. They were lost in the night's magic.

"Rusty, I love you," Victor whispered in her ear as they moved around the small dance floor.

"I love you, too, Victor."

"Will you come home with me? Will you spend the night with me?" Victor pressed her body against his.

His heat sent shock waves through her. She tilted her head back, looking into his eyes. "Yes, I'll spend the night with you."

Chapter 22

___

VICTOR LAY IN BED cradling Rusty as she slept. It had been a wonderful evening, and a spectacular night, better than he could have imagined. From what little Rusty had told him over the past months, he surmised that she was a virgin and that turned out to be true. He made love to her slowly, tenderly, waiting for her to respond to his touches. When neither one could hold back another second his body exploded in molten heat—she matched and then exceeded his passion.

What a wonderful woman, he thought, pulling her into his body, holding her against him. He loved Rusty but loved her drive for fame and fortune more. He knew his clinic would never bring in the money that Rusty's ranch was destined to make, and it didn't hurt that she was a beautiful woman. He was a lucky man to have her as she screamed out her love for him. Yes, everything was going as he planned. He hoped he could move in with her before the Albuquerque show next month so they could spend even more time together. He believed she would want this, especially after last tonight. He would then ask her to marry him.

They wanted the same thing—money, lots of money, more than he would ever be able to garner from his clinic. Yes, he would become part of her life. Yes, move in with her on that ranch. She would soon be rolling in dough. He would close his clinic and spend his time selecting Arabs while she grew the business, and if a horse needed a little help to remove a flaw, well so be it. With his skills as an equine surgeon, and her business acumen and training expertise, and the fact that clients were mesmerized with her beauty—doing whatever she suggested, he suggested—there was no stopping them.

Yes, Victor. You are a lucky man, all that and a beautiful woman on your arm. And if she becomes too busy for you, or you tire of her, well a discreet liaison now and then would certainly be acceptable, a little bend in the rules now and then. She would never notice if I was gone a few hours, or on a quick trip somewhere to check out a horse for her. Yes, it's all going to work. Life is good. He gently leaned in, nuzzled her ear.

Rusty felt his kiss and sleepily nestled closer, closer into his warm body.

Chapter 23

—

ONCE IN A WHILE BURNS thought back to the day, tired of corporate life in Phoenix, he left his job and invested his savings, along with the inheritance from his father, on a farm in Black Canyon City. He didn't know much about farming, nothing really, but he and his wife Henrietta had talked about moving away from the city to the desert in the shadows of the mountains they loved as children. Burns asked around for a lead on a manager for his new property, someone who loved the land as much as he did, but who also knew about cattle. After several people suggested the same man, a Navajo who had just sold his property, Burns went looking for him. It seemed the people he spoke with all said the same thing—check the bar at the other end of town.

Yuma was a broken young man sitting at the end of the bar the day Charles Burns came looking for him. The Indian had sold his small spread, no longer able to stay in the house where his wife died in childbirth. Two days after his wife died the baby girl left this earth to join her mother.

Burns found the Indian in the bar. He invited Yuma out to his spread the next day. He told him if they came to an understanding, that there was a little cottage on the edge of Canyon Creek that ran through the farm. The cottage would be his if he decided to live on the farm. Burns hoped Yuma would take him up on his offer.

—

YUMA ACCEPTED THE JOB and moved into the cottage. When six months later, Henrietta presented Charles with a robust, baby girl with red hair, Yuma felt he was blessed. *The gods sure do work in wondrous ways,* he thought. On the edge of despair only a few months back, he now lived in a little house that suited his needs. He had a boss who told him that if the farm did well under his guidance that he would prosper as well. And then came a baby girl to watch over.

That was thirty-one years ago, and here he stood in the little barn on the back of the property, tears streaming down his face as he applied ointment to the eyes of Moon Beam. The silvery-white mare was closed in her stall, barn doors shut tight. Only a sliver of light penetrated the wall through a crack between two of the old boards on the far side.

Victor had requested Yuma's assistance with the procedure he had performed on the sedated mare—the injection of a black inky substance into the whites of her eyes, and then tattooing a sliver of pink skin around each eye to a dark brown. Victor, packing his instruments back into his bag, had told Yuma what needed to be done to care for the mare—a couple of weeks in isolation, as dark as possible, until the eyes healed. Yuma knew that Victor was pleased with his work and overheard him tell Rusty that the mare's dark eyes against her beautiful silvery coat would surely win her a championship in October. He added that the prince would not be able to resist her beauty.

Yuma wiped his tears on his blue denim shirt as Moon Beam nuzzled his arm looking for her treat.

"Yes, pretty girl, give me a second to get it out of my pocket." The horse answered with a soft whinny as Yuma withdrew a carrot. Moon Beam gently took the carrot from his fingers and Yuma backed out of her stall, swinging the stall gate shut. He stood watching her chew the carrot—their eyes locked on each other.

Suddenly, Yuma couldn't stand looking at her. He rushed from the barn, picked up the bridle's reins on his mustang and, not waiting to saddle him, jumped on his back. With a couple of clucks from his mouth, Knight Rider took off. Yuma kept clucking, urging the Mustang on through the pastures, jumping over low fences, on and on, up into the hills until horse and rider exhausted came to a stop high on a plateau overlooking the valley floor.

Yuma slid off Knight Rider's back into a heap. Lifting his head, he could just make out the skyline of downtown Phoenix—the tall buildings, the planes lined up in the sky for their final approach into Phoenix Sky Harbor Airport. Moving his head slightly to the left he saw the eastern mountain range where Scottsdale nestled between the peaks.

Looking over his beloved native land, the answer to his dilemma came to him. He straightened his body. His lungs filled with the fresh mountain air. He threw his shoulders back, held his head high. He would talk to Charles. He had to let him know the extent of what was going on in the barns. Even more so since Victor had moved in with the Burns, and into Rusty's bed. Let him know that horses were being cut for no good reason. That they felt the pain long after the sedation wore off. That because Rusty rushed their training some wounds, not fully healed, had torn open. That he could not stay in a place where he felt the horses were undergoing operations when nothing was wrong with them.

If Burns couldn't stop what was happening, then he, Yuma, had no choice but to leave the ranch that he dearly loved.

Chapter 24

YUMA NUDGED KNIGHT RIDER with his knee—the mustang turned and headed for home. As the horse loped down the hillside to the desert floor, Yuma went over in his mind what he was going to say to Burns, and what he would do if Burns chose to ignore the disfigurement, in his mind anyway, that was being perpetrated on some of the horses. Spotting his hat, Yuma pulled up on the reins. Sliding off of Knight Rider's back, Yuma retrieved his old hat entangled in a ring of tumbleweeds, the sweatband stained from years of hard work. He mounted the gelding and urged him on, now at a gallop.

Yuma was ready.

Returning to the ranch he rubbed Knight Rider down and gave him a much needed drink of water.

Then it was time.

Yuma strode up to the back door, pushed the button ringing the bell as usual, and entered the Burns' home. Theresa, bent over the open oven door, was basting a turkey. She looked up as Yuma walked in. Before she could say hello, Yuma asked her if Mr. Burns was in his study. Seeing the determined look on Yuma's face seemed to cancel any thought she might have had to joke around or even offer him a glass of iced tea. She nodded yes to his question and went back to basting the turkey.

Yuma removed his weather-beaten rancher's hat and walked down the open hallway, bordered on one side by the living room and a gallery wall on the other. The wall was covered with photos and paintings of Rusty, her Arabs, and even a couple of himself branding a calf shortly after he had arrived on the ranch. He knew what he was going to say to his boss, and he was also aware that his days of walking down this corridor might be numbered.

The office door was open. Burns sat at his desk bent over the keyboard of his computer, fingers poised. He appeared to be thinking about what he wanted to type next. Yuma rapped once on the door jamb and entered. Looking up, Burns smiled at the sight of his ranch manager and friend. Clicking the save button, he rose and walked to Yuma, his arm extended for a friendly handshake.

"I was just writing you a note about a black Angus I saw yesterday. What do you think about adding him to our stock? Here, Yuma, have a seat. Iced tea?" Not waiting for his reply Burns flicked on the intercom and asked Theresa to bring in a pitcher of tea, some ice and two glasses. He then sat down and turned to face his friend. It was only then that Charles looked at Yuma and saw the concern etched in the lines on the Indian's face. "Yuma? What's the matter?"

"Mr. Burns, I talked to you a while ago about a procedure Victor had performed on one of the Arabs."

"Yes, yes, I remember. Victor made a small incision in the neck of a stallion, I believe. He removed a lump, a small amount of fatty tissue. I talked to Rusty about it."

"Well, sir, things are going on in the barn, surgeries, that I feel you need to know about ... and other procedures."

Theresa hustled into the room, set the tray with glasses, a small china dish of lemon wedges and a pitcher of tea with the ice cubes floating on top, on the coffee table between the two men. "Anything else you gentleman would like?" she asked wiping her hands on her white bib apron.

"No, this will do nicely, Theresa. Thank you," Burns said. Theresa left the room, closing the door behind her, allowing the two men some privacy.

Burns picked up where Yuma had been interrupted. "What other procedures?" Burns asked.

"You'll have to go to the barn to see for yourself to understand my concern."

"I talked to Rusty about the lump you said Victor removed." Charles handed a glass of tea to Yuma, who shook his head, no.

Charles put a couple of lemon wedges in the glass and leaned forward, elbows on his knees, trying to comprehend why Yuma was so worried. "She told me, it was a very small lump. She wanted to make sure it wasn't cancer. She told me it proved to be some fatty tissue that Victor removed. So you see, Yuma, as she explained it to me, it was a medical procedure. I mean, if it had been cancer—"

"Sir, with all due respect, there was never a question of that lump being cancerous. However, let's say Victor thought it might be and that's why he went in. But the final straw was yesterday."

"What happened yesterday?"

"That mare, Moon Beam. Rusty is schooling her for the show plus she wants to include her in the group for this Sultan person."

"Go on." Charles set his glass down on the tray. He was becoming alarmed at the depth of his friend's concern. Indians have a strong affinity and love for horses, so he had to separate Yuma's anxiety over potential harm from his love of the animals.

"Victor removed the whites of her eyes ... filling it with a black substance that looked like ink, and ... he tattooed the pink lining so the mare's eyes will appear bigger and all black."

"That is extreme." Charles stood up, paced back and forth a few steps, stopped, looked into Yuma's eyes, then paced to the large picture window. He could see the barns from this vantage point. Neither man spoke. He thought about what his wife had told him. *"Don't you do anything to spoil Rusty's dream."*

Charles turned away from the window. "Rusty said it was nothing. Her words, 'really nothing.' I'll go to the barn. See for myself." He turned back to the window. "Yes, I'll see for myself."

Having done what he came to do, Yuma left Charles, walked out to the kitchen, and on out the back door into the warm September sun. Stopping at the paddock, he put the bridle over Knight Rider's head, and again with no saddle, swung his body up on the gelding's back galloping off to his cottage. There was one last chore he had to do before checking out the Black Angus for Burns.

Tethering his horse to a post in the shade, Yuma entered the little house and strode into the spare bedroom he used as an office. He turned on his computer and while it was starting up, he pulled his little camera from his pocket. He looked at the camera a moment, knowing what it held—it looked small and insignificant in his leathered palm. The computer now ready, Yuma opened his desk drawer and retrieved the USB cable he needed to attach the camera to the computer in order to download the latest pictures. He watched the fifteen pictures he had taken of Moon Beam that morning flash in front of his dark brown eyes, squinting as they did so. The download finished leaving the last picture up on the screen—Moon Beam staring back at him with her big black eyes. Yuma stared at her a moment, then browsed through a few of the folders he had setup on the computer—over a hundred images in all.

After Victor removed the fatty tissue during the first operation, Yuma had made it his business to take a picture of each horse Rusty accepted on the ranch. It seemed every owner in the valley wanted her to train and groom their Arabs for the upcoming show. After the first operation Yuma wasn't sure if Victor would perform additional surgeries, alterations, but if he did a picture was stored of the horse in its original condition. Then methodically, as Victor performed an operation, Yuma would snap pictures of the aftercare—the hot packs, the bandages, and the incisions covered by the bandages. He wasn't sure what he would do with the photos, but his old Indian instinct said taking the pictures, keeping a record of what was happening at the Burns' ranch, was something he should do. The time would come when the gods would tell him when to print them.

Chapter 25

———

LIZ LOOPED MAGGIE'S LEASH over a hook on the fence post, gave her a pat on the head, and then walked to the entrance of the equine center. Maggie lay down on the soft grass but kept her head up looking at a foal and its mother in the paddock about twenty feet away.

Leslie glanced up from her computer and smiled as Liz walked in, a spring closing the door behind her.

"Hi, Leslie. Is Linda around? I told her I'd be by this morning."

"She sure is. Let me give a shout to the barn." Leslie pressed a code on the small console. "Liz is here, Linda ... will do. She'll be right up."

"Thanks. Leslie. Would you mind telling me again what you saw the morning Rick died? Can we go into the examination room?"

"Okay." Leslie led the way into the examination room propping the door open in case the phone rang.

"I found him lying in the middle of the floor here, here where I'm standing. The cart over there, with the ultrasound equipment, was tipped over. All the stuff Linda uses for examinations—containers of lubricant, plastic bags to shield her hand and arms when she inserts the wand into the mare's rectum for the ultrasound reading, and her laptop computer—were scattered on the floor. His leg was actually on top of the laptop. He must have been in terrible pain. His hands were clutching his shirt, kinda his chest."

"Was he lying on his back or his side?"

"His side, I guess you'd say."

"Would you say he was in the fetal position?"

"Yes, yes, exactly."

The door from the stall area swung open as Andy led a horse into the metal-railed stock to be examined, closing the gate behind the mare. Linda followed her husband, close on his heels.

"Hi, Liz," they both said in unison, chuckling. Both wore jeans tucked into black rubber boots, ready to perform the mare's examination.

"Hi. I was just going over with Leslie how she found Rick that morning," Liz said.

"I'm going out front. Let me know if you need anything else," Leslie said.

"Thanks, Leslie." Liz turned back to Linda and Andy. "I just can't get it out of my mind the pain he must have suffered with the combination of the cocaine and then the taser shot."

"We know what you mean," Linda said. "Andy and I still puzzle over it. I think Detective Milhous feels the same way, or maybe not. He asked for the name of Rick's doctor. Of course, we had no clue if he even had a doctor. His mom and dad thought he was being treated for some kind of virus trying to explain away the coke as a kind of medication. By the way, Liz, I was talking to Jerry Stevens and he mentioned your name. He said you were investigating or trying to find his stolen mare."

"That's right and that's a question I had for you guys. If the people who took her knew she was carrying a foal, would they seek advice from a vet, you know, for her care?"

"Oh, I hope they would," Andy piped up.

"You didn't get any calls in response to your emails with Desiree's picture though." Liz looked up at Linda. "Did you?"

Linda shook her head. "Would've been nice, but no."

"Can I get a list of the vets you sent the notice to and anybody else who might have been included? I'm going to visit a few, see if I can turn up something."

"Ask Leslie. She'll print out the names and I'm sure she has the email addresses and street addresses." Linda rolled her eyes at the distinction she had to make because of the computer.

"Linda, what is the vet's name in Jacksonville. Given he already has a tie with Stevens, I definitely want to see if he had any inquiries about looking after a pregnant horse."

"Harold Wilder. He's had his center for quite a while. Now if you'll excuse me, I can see that Sunny here is becoming impatient. Get what you need from Leslie and let me know if you find anything."

Linda pulled on a long plastic bag over her hand and arm, reaching up over her shoulder, then grabbed a hand full of lubricant and started her examination of the horse.

———

LIZ STOPPED TO FILL up on gas before driving to the next vet clinic. The list Leslie had given her was a combination of veterinarians with only a few specializing or devoted solely to horses. She'd visited several clinics, giving out posters with Desiree's picture. All the equine vets had the mare's picture tacked to a bulletin board, but the vets serving mainly cats and dogs hardly had time to talk to her let alone put up a poster. They gave Liz the go ahead to add Desiree to their gallery of missing pet postings if she wanted. She wanted, and then drove on.

She'd been on the road for five hours and stopped at Mickey D's for a burger. She was so hungry that Maggie was treated to her own burger instead of sharing a few bites from her mistress's lunch. With a fresh cup of coffee in hand, Liz headed east on Route 10 to Jacksonville and the vet that Stevens had contracted with to store Black Magic's frozen straws of semen.

Arriving a little after four o'clock, she found the reception area deserted. However, at the sound of the buzzer when she opened the front door, a man, Liz guessed to be in his fifties, walked in from an opposite door. His hair was graying, shoulder length, covering his ears. He hiked up his jeans almost covering his scruffy boots and dusted off his black T-shirt with his hands.

"What can I do for you, little lady?"

Liz moved back a step getting a whiff of the liquor on his breath. "I'm looking for Dr. Wilder."

"Well now, I can help you, or maybe not. It depends on if you want the junior or senior version. The senior would be your best bet. That would be me." Dr. Harold Wilder sat down behind the reception desk. "It's Friday, closing time, so me and the boys just had us a little happy hour. It's a ritual on Friday afternoon. Would you like to join us?"

"No, I don't think so, maybe another Friday. I'm actually on my way home. I've been out looking at horses and a friend, Mr. Jerry Stevens, I think you know him, suggested I stop by."

Wilder sat up straight and seemed to Liz to suddenly be all business instead of funny business. "Hell, why didn't you say you were a friend of Stevens. If there's something you want to know about horses, I'm your man."

"Actually, Dr. Wilder, I promised Jerry that everywhere I stopped I would drop off a poster of Desiree, a mare of his that was stolen a few weeks ago. Have you been to Jerry's farm? You might have seen her." Liz pulled out a copy of the poster. In gazing around the lobby area she did not see a copy even though there was plenty of wall space where Wilder could have taped one up.

Wilder took the poster. Studied it. "No, I don't believe anyone brought this mare to my clinic. But if she was stolen what makes you think I might have seen her?"

"She's carrying a foal, about eight months along now. I've been asking other vets hoping she may have been brought in to be checked, you know pregnant and all. Linda Turner made up the poster."

"Linda Turner. Well now, there's a fine vet. You know her, too?"

"Oh, yes. Seems like when you talk about horses, especially Arabs, it's a pretty tight circle. This is quite a place you have. Can I see the stalls?"

"You certainly can, miss. Just follow me ... watch your step though. The boys haven't exactly washed up everything yet today."

The two walked through the exam area and then out the back of the building. Wilder's setup was similar to Linda's—stalls off of the examination room.

Liz saw a barn about fifty yards away. "What about that one?" she asked pointing to the structure.

"Just some empty stalls," Wilder said. "You tell Jerry Stevens that if I see his mare, I'll certainly let him know ... right away."

"I'm sure he'll appreciate that. Well, I'd better get going. The traffic will be brutal this time of day. Nice chatting with you and keep the poster. I'd appreciate it if you put it up on your wall. I'm sure Jerry would thank you as well."

Liz pulled out of the yard and turned west onto I-10. She took a sip of her cold coffee and returned it to the beverage holder. Maggie was curled up on the passenger seat, and Liz absentmindedly stroked her head, careful to keep up with traffic.

"Maggie, that was a strange visit. I guess the doc was nice enough. I think he started his Friday happy hour a little early, but what the heck. It's a tough business. I've certainly seen Linda when she could hardly put one foot in front of the other. But why wouldn't he have put up the poster? Not only was he on the list Leslie gave me but his name was circled. Oh, well, I'm so tired I just want to get home and into a hot bath. Maybe even a glass of wine—my own happy hour, like old Doc Wilder."

Chapter 26

——

CLIMBING OUT OF HER CAR with Maggie in tow, Liz strolled up to the Stevens' barn.

"Jerry, you here?" she called.

"Sure am," he called out. "Come on down to Magic's stall. I'm brushing his coat. It won't be long and we'll be on our way to New Mexico."

"So soon? I thought the show was still three weeks away?"

Jerry stuck his head out over the stall gate, a curry brush in his hand. "That's right, but I'll start out in seven to ten days. I have friends along the way, horse friends with farms. They'll be putting us up—nice way to break up the trip for Magic. I'm glad you stopped by," he said showing an easy smile. "Did you visit some vets last week? I know you said that was your plan."

"My plan, as you call it, lasted over six hours."

"Turn up anything?" Jerry backed Black Magic up a few steps and continued grooming him.

"Sorry to say, I didn't. All the vets but two had the posters tacked up on a wall. The first was a general vet—no room on the bulletin boards—wall-to-wall dogs and cats in the waiting room. But the second one without a poster was rather a surprise— Wilder's clinic in Jacksonville."

"Ah, so you met him. Kind of a character."

"That's one way to put it. I don't know, Jerry, I had an uneasy feeling about him."

"Well, he was highly recommended by my friend. I visited his clinic to check it out, and, of course, to talk to him personally. He is a bit unorthodox, but I thought he ran a tight operation. The storage facility for the straws was state-of-the-art and we signed the papers. He has some of the straws now, and I'm sending more—he and Linda will have about the same number. What did he do that bothered you?"

"I'm not saying he bothered me, well, maybe I am. Don't you think it's strange he didn't have Desiree's picture posted, I mean you storing Black Magic's straws there and all."

"Yea, I see your point." Jerry looked at Liz. "I'm sorry you didn't learn anything about Desiree. I had a bad dream—she lost her foal ... very unsettling." He turned back to Magic, rested his forehead on her neck. Straightening up, he said, "When I get back from New Mexico, I'll take a run up to Jacksonville. Check on things."

"Good."

"Now, I've got something I want to show you." Jerry stroked his horse's nose then stepped out of the stall. Reaching into his pocket he pulled out a piece of paper. "I got this letter yesterday in the mailbox."

"Wow, I didn't think people sent letters by snail-mail anymore." Liz took the paper from Jerry and read the letter as Jerry poured a scoop of grain into Magic's feed tray.

"Oh, oh. This doesn't sound good. No signature. Typed. It says a judge may be bought off and that you could run into trouble at the show. I hope you kept the envelope."

"Yep, right here." Jerry pulled a folded envelope out of his back pants pocket, handing it to Liz. "No return address."

"Postmark is Phoenix. Do you know the red-head it refers to? Says she would do almost anything to win a championship."

"I think so. I ran into her in Kentucky. One of the first shows I went to. Took one of my mares. I really just wanted to see what showing in the ring was all about before entering Magic. She was a judge for a couple of classes. I didn't notice anything out of the ordinary. Lots of buzz about her though."

"What kind of buzz."

"Just that she was a good groomer and did well with schooling Arabs. That she was aggressive when it came to her business, whatever that meant. Barbara and I talked her on the way home. We wished we had started raising Arabs when we were her age."

"How old do you put her?"

"Thirties, no more."

"Jerry, I'm going to fly to Albuquerque."

"You're what? What for?"

"Well, being my two favorite clients are in the horse business, I think I'd be smart to become familiar with that business. Of course, I do have some sleuthing ideas, especially after this letter. We can bump into each other, but other than that I want to observe without anyone tying you to me if you catch my drift."

"You sure do turn your words around, young lady. I promise I won't say a word to you unless it's by Morse code. I won't have time for socializing anyway. Barbara is staying home to field the calls for breeding services, just in case the big guy pulls off a championship. Tony's riding shotgun with me."

———

LIZ WAS ON HER WAY to meet David for lunch—at his invitation. She smiled as she walked from her office to Harry's on the city square. Enjoying the mild air on this first day of October, marking the end of the summer heat, she looked forward to seeing him other than on their morning jog. Lunch was almost like a date. Almost. David was waiting for her, sitting at a table in the corner. Liz suddenly remembered the drink she and Joe Rocket had shared a few weeks before—but the memory left as quickly as it had arrived. Her heart skipped a bit when David rose to greet her. He was dressed in his uniform, gun belt fully loaded with his shiny accessories.

"I ordered a couple of coffees. If you want something else I'll be glad to drink yours."

"Coffee is great, thanks. How's everything in your world, officer?" Liz cocked her head to the side looking at him with her large brown eyes and a broad smile."

"Not bad. Nobody killed anybody this morning, which always starts the day off right. How about you? Visit those vets?"

"Yep, over six-hours worth," she replied taking a sip of her coffee.

"Turn up anything?"

"I'm not sure, probably not. I stopped to see Jerry this morning, don't let me forget to tell you about a letter he received. Anyway, my last stop was the Wilder Equine Clinic in Jacksonville. He's the vet now storing half of Black Magic's frozen semen. You know, Jerry's insurance company said the price for the straws—"

"Excuse me. Straws?"

"Ha. Gotcha," Liz said, her face lighting up in amusement. "Black Magic's semen is frozen in straws—like a little soda straw. Just learning everything I can about my client, like a good little PI." Liz took a sip of coffee, enjoying the one-upmanship over her friend. "Anyway, I can't put my finger on it, but to say I was not impressed with Wilder would be an understatement. But Jerry says Wilder, and I quote, 'has a state-of-the-art facility.'" She filled David in on her visit with Wilder, stopping only to order Harry's Catfish Po Boy. David gave the waitress his order—Harry's Shrimp Taco.

Waiting for their lunch to be served, Liz asked David if there were any new leads on the taser and whether he found anything of interest on Rick's computer. Their lunch arrived and the waitress topped off their coffee mugs. David handed the empty sugar bowl to her and she returned with the bowl full of sugar packets.

"Any new leads ... now let me think."

"Come on, David. You said you wanted to talk to me when you suggested we meet for lunch today.

"Ah, Yes. Well, when I'm wrong I just want you to know I'm big enough to admit it."

"Go, big man—"

"It seems I remember a certain PI saying that she thought the intern case and the stolen mare were connected."

"Yes, I heard a certain PI say that." Liz leaned forward in her chair, watching David's face. "So, so—"

"Not so fast. And that same PI found a cigarette butt way out in a field and gave it to a detective to see if it matched a butt he found in a certain intern's kitchen sink. Are you with me so far?"

"Oh my God—they matched?"

"Yes, they did, my friend—beyond a reasonable doubt is how I believe the prosecutor will phrase it."

"Wow. I just wish we had the guy, or maybe it's a gal, who smoked that butt."

"Well, it wasn't Rick," David said, smiling at her over the rim of his coffee mug. *She's some pretty PI,* he thought. "Honest to God, Liz, it's as if nobody tased him, yet we know it happened. Talk about a case gone cold." David tore open a couple of sugar packets, dropping the contents into his coffee along with a good shot of cream. "You said something about a letter."

"Yes, it was weird. Came snail mail warning Stevens to watch out when he's in New Mexico. Next time you see him, ask him about it. Anyway, I'm going to fly to Albuquerque in a couple of weeks."

"Albuquerque?"

"Yes. Call it field work."

"You be careful, now, you hear? Take your cell phone … call me. I don't want anything to happen to my favorite jogging companion."

Liz looked up and smiled, "Yes, Daddy." Her stomach lurched and she knew it wasn't from the Po Boy. She also noticed that her pulse quickened whenever she saw David. She was beginning to look forward to seeing him in the morning with Whiskey, timing her jog to his, and their conversations, even if they were only about their cases.

Chapter 27

―――

RUSTY HAD STEPPED UP the schooling and grooming of the six horses she was transporting to Albuquerque's Fair Grounds. She planned their arrival in New Mexico four days before the show to get her horses settled into their stalls and resting before competition began.

With the horses finally loaded, the caravan pulled away from the barn. Yuma was driving a trailer of four following Rusty and Victor. Her truck pulled a trailer with two horses, one being Sampson. Yuma was to remain at the Fair Grounds throughout the show to help her. Rusty was listed in the program as a judge for three classes.

Charles, Henry, and Theresa waved them on with wishes of good luck as the trucks drove down the driveway, through the gate, and onto the highway heading east.

―――

TRUCKS, SUV'S AND ASSORTED other vehicles, all with horse trailers hitched to the back end, were lined up waiting to be checked in and assigned barns and stalls. Windows were rolled down letting in the soft, warm breezes from the dry New Mexico air. It was almost show time—four more days until the first class would kickoff the event. The only thing the owners wanted to do now was to unload their horses so the animals could rest. A loudspeaker barked out instructions but there was no honking of horns in agitation over the slow pace of the check-in process. All this happened the day before the big glut would occur. Tomorrow was the day when most of the show participants were expected to arrive.

Rusty had witnessed the chaos before, so she, Victor, and Yuma had arrived before dawn and were now settled in the barn.

"You guys want some coffee?" Rusty asked, pushing a trunk filled with the gear they would need for the show next to the wall of Sampson's stall.

"Yes, babe. That would be great—make it a large," Victor said.

"Count me in," Yuma said. "I'll drive the trucks to the parking lot. You have everything unloaded?" he asked Victor.

"Yep, go ahead."

Rusty, wiping her hands on her jeans, headed for the coffee concession. Standing in line, she felt a tap on her shoulder.

"Are you Miss Burns?" the man asked.

She turned to face the man. He touched the brim of his hat in greeting.

"Clyde, you know who I am. How many horses do you have entered this year?" Rusty stepped forward to the front of the line and ordered three coffees, all black.

"Can I talk to you a minute, Rusty?"

"Sure. Let me pay first. Want a cup?"

"No thanks. I'll wait for you over there by that tree."

Rusty followed with the coffees in a cardboard-cup tray.

"So, Clyde, I haven't seen you in a while." Rusty sat down next to the man. Like almost everyone at the show, he wore jeans over cowboy boots, a long-sleeve shirt, bolo tie with a turquoise stone, and a black-felt Stetson covering his dark-brown hair. Rusty could tell by his no-nonsense manner that this was not a social visit.

"It has been a while, over a year in fact, since you showed me a picture of a filly yearling you thought should win a regional championship, or a reserve anyway. I was a judge for her class."

"That's right," Rusty replied. "I was grateful you agreed with me. Very grateful."

"Yes. The wife and I enjoyed the week we spent in Aruba after the show. Very kind of you to arrange it for us."

"Get to the point, Clyde. These coffees are getting cold."

"Well now, looking at the program, I have a stallion scheduled to show on the second day and you are listed as a judge. See, I have it right here, Rusty Burns."

"Yes, I'll be one of the judges."

"Here, let me show you a picture of Diamond Prince." Clyde pulled out a picture of a bay Arab stallion, a large white blaze on his forehead shaped like a star.

"He is a beauty—looks like a winner," Rusty said giving the picture back to Clyde.

"Do you think so? Oh, I must tell you ... my wife and I were going to Nice this spring, but she doesn't think we can make it. A shame really—the hotel is on the beach, a suite of rooms ... all paid for. Do you like France, Rusty?"

"As a matter of fact I do, especially in the spring."

Clyde looked at the picture of his horse again. "So you think he looks like a winner?"

"I'm sure of it."

Chapter 28

———

JERRY WAS BACK ON THE ROAD, his truck pulling the trailer with Black Magic. Tony sat in the seat beside him—both men sipping coffee they picked up at the last stop for gas. Jerry had figured the trip would take four days and three nights. His timing was right on. The turnoff for the Albuquerque Fair Grounds was just ahead.

The scene was chaotic. Trailers drew up to the barns. Trainers, owners, helpers scampered to unload their horses, along with all of the gear they needed to bathe, groom, and show them—including saddles, blankets, bridles, and halters.

After checking in, Jerry and Tony bathed Magic and then settled him in his stall to rest up for the show.

Because of the threatening letter, Jerry had hired his own security guard to be sure his horse was never left alone. However, Tony said he was going to stay close to the stall, maybe even sleep in the barn. Once Black Magic was safely in his stall Jerry left to register at his hotel. Black Magic wasn't the only one who needed to rest. Jerry was exhausted from the strain of the trip, hauling his precious cargo, as well as trying to tamp down his excitement at being a participant at this premier show.

Friday was another hectic day. Horses being led around the exercise paddocks; horses being bathed in cement stalls complete with hose hookup and drain. Shouts of, "hi," "nice to see you," and "good luck," were heard, or not, depending on the announcements blaring over the loudspeakers. Organized chaos.

Jerry looked over the schedule for events where Rusty Burns was listed as a judge. The scuttlebutt in the barn was to watch out for her. "You don't want to cross her," was said by more than one handler.

———

THE FIRST CLASS OF THE afternoon was announced and the horses were queuing up to enter the ring. At the last minute Jerry was approached by a frantic trainer. The man had two horses entered into the event. He was showing a gelding but the handler presenting the mare didn't show up. He asked Jerry to show the mare. He agreed, but because Jerry wasn't a professional handler, he had to show his credentials when signing the registration sheet as the handler for the horse before entering the ring. Once in the ring, the judges appeared to be questioning something and then he was instructed over the loudspeaker to sign-in again.

What's this all about, Jerry thought. Leading the mare out of the ring he glanced over at the judges wondering who raised the fuss. He locked eyes with the Burns woman. She raised her chin slightly and turned away. *Game on,* he thought.

At the check-in table, Jerry raised a mild protest. The mare placed third. Jerry thought she was a superior horse compared with the other two and should have placed higher. Of the five judges, three, including Burns, had scored the winner. *Maybe she was bought off,* Jerry thought.

He watched another event Burns judged that went against the horse she had chosen. He witnessed a brouhaha between the five judges after the event. He was relieved to note on the program that she was not judging the class in which Black Magic was entered. Jerry felt his horse had a good chance to survive the elimination and move on to the finals. Even though Burns wasn't judging the event, she was showing a stallion. *So,* Jerry thought, *we're going to be bumping up against each other in the ring.*

———

JERRY INHALED A DEEP BREATH. "Okay, boy, it's show time."

There were twenty-five horses entered in the class. Jerry was ninth in line as he and Magic entered the ring. If you were a spectator, it was a breathtaking display of the finest Arabians in the world. If you were a handler, it was nerve-racking.

With all the horses in the ring the head judge, with the aid of a microphone, called out her instructions.

"Trot please."

"Walk."

"Reverse direction."

"Stand up."

At this command, each handler stood-up his horse: head up, legs square under his body. The five judges walked around each animal making notes on their clipboards, ranking all twenty-five in a twenty-point system. Twenty being picture perfect.

As the judges continued to scrutinize the horses, they scribbled on their sheets, moving a horse up or down in ranking. Jerry knew Black Magic had to rank in the top ten in order to move to the next round in the competition. He kept whispering to Magic, "Good, boy. Keep your head up now ... that's it. Stand still."

The judges congregated, tallied up the points, made adjustments to their list—changing the order of their choices, then merged their selections together.

The lead judge then systematically walked to a handler, said a few words, and the horse was led out of the ring. The elimination proceeded until only ten horses remained in the ring.

Jerry kissed the side of Magic's nose—he was still standing in the ring. Jerry looked down the line at the other nine horses. Rusty Burns was also in the ring with her stallion.

It was now time for the judges to pick the Champion and the Reserve Champion.

The show was in high gear—the arena filled to capacity. A few spectators stood by the four-foot high iron railing bordering the entrance into the ring to cheer on their favorite. Some, who were connected to a horse in the ring, made a loud clucking sound perking up their horse when he heard the noise—ears forward as they pranced pounding their hooves into the dirt.

A hush fell over the spectators as Jerry paraded Black Magic around the ring. It seemed they knew they were witnessing an elegant Arab, if not perfection itself. Jerry followed the judge's orders, "walk your horse ... trot please ... reverse direction." The head judge finally ordered the horses to stand up. The handlers one-by-one lined up their horses, and struck a pose—legs straight, hooves anchored to the dirt floor, strong and straight, heads erect, ears up, tails flagging.

Again the judges walked around each horse, looking for flaws, checking conformation, then marking their score sheets, shuffling one horse ahead or behind another.

After several minutes, the judges congregated back at their table, tallying up the points they awarded each horse. Again they merged their individual findings, agreeing on the champion, and the placement of the remaining horses in the group. As before, the head judge approached a handler, spoke a few words, and then the handler led his horse out of the ring. He had been eliminated. Seven horses left the ring—three remained: Black Magic, Rusty's stallion, and one other. The head judge handed the final placements to the announcer who boomed the results over the loudspeaker.

"U.S. National Arabian Champion is Black Magic. U.S. National Arabian Reserve Champion is Prince Sampson."

Jerry threw his arms around the neck of his friend, and then quickly stood back as the judges formed a line to shake his hand and pet the neck of the champion.

The head judge, a broad smile on her face, spoke a few words to Jerry. "Why don't you parade Black Magic around the ring. I think his fans would appreciate seeing him strut his stuff."

"Thanks, I will." Jerry, his face beaming said to his stallion, "Come on boy, let's give 'em a show."

Jerry started to run over the dirt floor of the ring, arm outstretched holding the lead in his hand. Black Magic held his head high, ears forward, hooves prancing. The crowd went wild—loving the show. Black Magic not only won the judges score but the hearts of the crowd as well.

Chapter 29

———

A JUBILANT JERRY STEVENS led the champion Arabian from the ring and was immediately encased by a throng of people wanting to see the stallion up close—petting his nose, snapping pictures, and asking questions. Black Magic stood quietly taking the mayhem in stride.

Tony, squeezing through the crowd, threw his arms around his boss and then hugged Magic.

"He did it. He won," Tony shouted over the loudspeaker announcing a dressage class.

"Tony, here, hold him a minute," Jerry said handing him the lead attached to Magic's halter. "I have to call Barbara."

The loudspeaker boomed again announcing more classes in the outdoor rings.

"Barb, he won," Jerry shouted into his cell phone over the noise.

"What? I can't hear you."

"He won. He won!"

"He won? Oh my God, Jerry. He won!"

The loudspeaker cut out as Jerry shouted again, "Yes, he won."

The crowd around him laughed still taking pictures, admiring the winner. Someone asked Tony who they should call about breeding services. Slowly Tony led Magic away from the group that was gathering so Jerry could continue his conversation with his wife.

"Call Linda, will you? After I get Magic settled back in his stall, Tony and I will be heading to the hotel to get some lunch."

"Jerry—"

"What's the matter? Did something happen?" The tone of Barbara's voice had suddenly changed from jubilation to, to what?

"Jerry, I had a call last night from Wilder ... I didn't want to upset you. I knew you'd be a little nervous today, but you need to know."

"What did Wilder say? You sound upset."

"There was a fire. Part of his clinic was destroyed."

"Is the storage facility okay?"

"Most of it."

"What do you mean most of it? Are Magic's straws okay? Barbara, please, you're holding back on me."

"The straws were destroyed."

"All of them."

"Yes. Destroyed. Wilder said he was sorry."

"Sorry. Sorry. Barbara, you're going to start getting calls from here. Black Magic won. Dealers and owners have already approached me, asking about stud fees. I was barely out of the ring. Call Linda. Tell her what happened at Harold Wilder's facility. Ask her if her storage unit is secure."

"I already did. She said to let you know someone would have to threaten her life before she'd give up any straws."

"Barbara, did Wilder say someone set the fire? Was it arson?"

"I didn't ask. I was too upset, but I'll call him back to find out."

"That's it—I'm heading home." Jerry was almost to the barn. Tony stood in the entrance still holding Magic for the last people to take his picture. He looked over at his beautiful horse. *Nothing is going to happen to you*, he thought. "The main event for Magic is over. There are mainly dressage and other riding classes left."

"Honey, I don't want you to miss the show. You traveled—"

"I'll stay the rest of today, but then Tony and I will pack up and leave for home in the morning." Jerry closed his cell. Rubbing his head, he looked around in a daze, the jubilation tarnished.

———

TONY STAYED IN THE BARN with Black Magic fielding questions from fans who stopped by to see the champion. Jerry went back to the hotel to take a shower, trying to settle his nerves. *How could Wilder let something like that happen,* he thought. As he stepped out of the shower, he heard the hotel phone ring. Grabbing a towel, he walked to the bedside table and answered on the third ring.

"Mr. Stevens, this is the concierge. A note was left for you earlier. It's marked urgent."

"Okay, I'm coming down for lunch. I'll pick it up on my way. Do you know who left it?"

"No. I found it when I came on duty a few minutes ago. The envelope is sealed—only your name and the word urgent ... underlined."

Jerry dressed quickly and headed for the concierge station. Identifying himself, he asked for the message that was being held for him and then walked briskly to the lunch buffet set up outside on the patio. Before joining the buffet line, he walked to the edge of the patio and sat down on a low flagstone wall bordering a profusion of flowering hibiscus bushes. He opened the envelope, slid out the cream-colored notepaper, and read the typed message: "Watch out Mr. Stevens. Someone may try to clip your horse's tail."

Jerry jammed the note back into the envelope, anger shooting from his eyes, jaw muscles tightening. He turned back to the bank of elevators, rode to his floor, and stormed into his room. Throwing his toiletries into the small bag, and his clothes into the suitcase, he returned to the front desk.

Within an hour of receiving the warning, he and Tony were on the highway heading east to Florida.

Chapter 30

———

PERCHED HIGH IN THE grandstand of the 4000-seat horse arena, Liz, watched as Black Magic became the U.S. National Champion. Her eyes misted with happiness as Jerry ran around the ring with the stallion for a victory lap. Her attention, however, was split between Black Magic and a tall, dark-haired man, mid to late thirties. Liz had observed the man earlier in an ardent embrace with Rusty Burns. Burns was about to lead a horse into the ring when Liz caught the scene.

After the announcement of the Champion and the Reserve Champion, Rusty's horse, the man edged near the gate area. But when Rusty left the ring with the stallion, she angrily brushed the man's hand off her arm and strutted off to the barn area. A few spectators moved next to her asking questions about Sampson and congratulating her on the Reserve designation. She did not stop to give them a response, leaving several indignant fans in her wake. Liz thought this might be a good time to learn about Burns from the scorned man.

"Oh, excuse me. I didn't mean to bump you. I'm so clumsy," the man said.

"No, it's my fault, really," Liz said shaking coffee off her hand.

"Look, I've caused you to spill your coffee," he said. "Here, take my handkerchief."

"Thank you, I did manage to keep it off my blouse," Liz said wiping the liquid from her fingers.

"The least I can do is buy you another coffee," he offered.

"Thanks, I'll take you up on that. I do need a pick-me-up. Here's your handkerchief but I'm afraid it's stained."

"Not a problem." The man took the cloth and threw it in the trash barrel next to the coffee concession.

"Cream? Sugar?"

"Black, please."

He paid for the coffee and handed her the hot cup. "This one has a lid to protect you from clumsy men," he said with a smile. "How about we grab one of those benches under that tree over there unless you were on your way somewhere?"

"No, not going anywhere. Just watching the competition."

"My name is Victor Bennett, and you are?"

"Elizabeth, Elizabeth Standish. Please, call me Liz."

"What brings you to the horse show, Elizabeth Standish, a boyfriend?"

"Heavens, no, whatever gave you that idea?" she said smiling into his eyes.

"Oh, I don't know. A pretty woman like you must have a boyfriend."

"Actually, I'm here by myself. Trying to learn something about Arabians. A few of my friends back home in Florida have started raising them, you know, on a farm. How about you? Are you showing a horse today?"

"No, no, I help out a local rancher. I'm a veterinarian."

"Well then, you really know all about these beasts. You can tell I don't know much. Do you have your own clinic?"

"I did. Closed it down recently. The ranch I mentioned seemed to need me more and more, so I'm pretty much full time out there. Say, how about meeting me for drinks later. The rancher is meeting a client for dinner and I'd be in the way. I can tell you more about the Arabians."

"That's an offer I'm definitely accepting, Victor. What time and where would you like to meet?"

"How about seven o'clock in the bar at the La Fiesta restaurant ... unless you don't like the Mexican version of a Margarita?"

"Only if the rim of the glass is salted. I saw the restaurant when I drove to my hotel. See you then."

———

"WHAT do you mean Jerry left?" Liz was back in the stands after accepting the drink date with Victor. The loudspeaker blared out the call for the horses to enter the ring for the next class—she wasn't sure she heard Barbara right.

"When he returned to the hotel after Magic's win, a note had been left for him, marked urgent. Liz, it was a threat watch out or, I'm quoting now, 'your horse's tail will be clipped.' It was too much for Jerry. So he and Tony packed up and they're on the road as we speak. But wait, there's more bad news."

"What else? Whatever it is it can't be worse than that note."

"I'm afraid it is. There was a fire at Wilder's—all of Magic's straws were destroyed."

"Oh my God, Barbara. That's awful. I can see why he left."

"That's not all. Almost immediately after Black Magic won the championship, calls started coming in—dealers and owners wanted to get on our breeding list. You'll never believe who just called me...Linda. She said someone had inquired about buying some straws directly from her. They were trying to bypass us, which is a no-no."

"Can you send me an email with any details you have about the fire or if Linda calls again. Ask Jerry if the note was signed ... probably wasn't. I'm going to stay, only until mid-afternoon tomorrow. I have a date to have drinks with Rusty Burns' veterinarian. Hopefully, I'll learn more about her. If Jerry tells you anything more you think I should know text or call me. Otherwise, I'll check in with you when I get back home."

———

THE RESTAURANT WAS ABLAZE with Tiki Torches and tiny white lights strung on bushes, small palms, and lattice partitions between the tables giving the guests some privacy. Victor was sitting at the bar when Liz walked in. He spotted her first and rose to greet her.

"Hey, you look beautiful."

"Thanks. It's a lovely evening. I'm beginning to appreciate why people fall in love with the southwest. Does the desert always glow like this when the sun is setting?"

"In Phoenix, yes. Here, it seems so as well—another paradise," He said with a smile. "I reserved a table for us. Excuse me while I check in with the hostess."

They were seated in a cozy nook shielded by bushy plants and two votives in the center of the table. They each placed a drink order with the waiter.

"Have you lived in Arizona long?" Liz asked.

"Born and raised. Can't imagine living anywhere else. You should see it when the desert flowers are in full bloom."

Their drinks came along with crispy tortilla chips and hot salsa for dipping. The waiter asked if they were staying for dinner. Victor raised his eyebrows questioning whether Liz would accept the invitation. She nodded, yes.

The evening proceeded both enjoying each other's company; at least Liz hoped that's what Victor thought. When he started on his third Margarita, she guided the conversation to his work on the Burns' ranch.

"To have a full-time vet, they must have a lot of horses," Liz said.

"It depends. Rusty schools horses for clients so they can show them, or she shows them. We do some breeding and, of course, that's when I step in. Rusty will match a stallion in the valley with a mare and I do the insemination, collection first, of course."

"What else do you do?" Liz took a sip of her wine that she had nursed throughout dinner.

"Oh, treat injuries, watch their diet ... but the real interesting part is if surgery is required."

"Surgery."

"Well, yea, nothing really. Maybe remove a lump."

"A lump?"

"Could be cancerous, you know."

"I see. That wouldn't be good." Finishing her drink, Liz said, "Victor, I think I'd better be getting back to my hotel. It's been a long day." Liz said.

"How about we exchange email addresses?" Victor asked writing his address on a cocktail napkin and sliding it over to her.

"Okay, you never know, I may need some more information on the Arabians."

Liz had learned a trick from Goodwurthy—always be ready with an extra email address so you don't blow your cover. Tearing the napkin in half, she wrote her alias email address for Elizabeth Standish and handed it to him.

Victor flagged the waiter and paid the bill. Liz walked through the aisle which meandered around the tables to the front door. A soft breeze fluttered through the bushes giving the illusion that the little white lights were twinkling. At her rental car, Liz turned to say goodnight. Victor leaned in and kissed her with more passion than a first date warranted. She slipped out of his embrace.

"Victor, thank you for dinner but we just met, I barely know you."

"We can take care of that." He reached for her, but in his slightly inebriated condition he missed and stumbled against the car.

Liz quickly stepped into the car and started the engine. "Thanks again" she called out through the open window and sped out of the parking lot to the street.

The next day she didn't catch sight of Victor until late morning. Liz had changed her plane ticket that morning feeling she had seen enough. She walked away from the ring and down a grassy slope to the path leading to the parking lot. As she approached her car she saw that Victor was leaning against the passenger-side door.

"Hello, beautiful," he said. "How about lunch?"

"Tempting, but no can do. I'm off to the airport."

As she passed the front of the car, he gently took hold of her arm and turned her to him. She maneuvered in such a way he only landed a kiss on her cheek. Again, she quickly got into the car. *Making a quick getaway is getting to be a habit,* she thought. "Bye, Victor." She waved at him through the closed window and made a beeline for the airport.

Victor didn't see Rusty standing at the crest of the hill overlooking the parking lot. She was on her way back to the barn when she saw Victor leaning up against a car.

Chapter 31

⸺

THE MOST IMPORTANT ITEM on Rusty's agenda was to return to Arizona and prepare for her upcoming meeting with Prince Sultan Al Amri at the Burns Arabian Horse Ranch and to finalize a five-million-dollar sale—a steal. She had priced the four horses at a bargain hoping to attain her goal of becoming a player on the world market for Arabians.

When the show began she looked up the prince and gave him a program with the classes circled where she was showing a horse she hoped Sultan would buy. They would be at their best prancing in the ring. She knew it was a gamble that they might not place, but one she was willing to take. Her luck held—they all placed in the top three slots of their competition including the Reserve Champion—Sampson. At dinner, she had given him pictures of the horses reminding him of their beauty until he saw them up close in a few days when he traveled to Arizona and her ranch.

Now, finished with her business at the Albuquerque show, she was packing up for the trip home and her meeting with the prince. She and Yuma had loaded the first two horses into the trailer when Victor rounded the corner of the barn. He helped Yuma load the remaining four when Rusty abruptly left driving her truck down the access road. Victor jumped in the cab of the truck with Yuma, and the little caravan headed west to Arizona. If Victor thought it strange that Rusty didn't say a word to him, he didn't indicate it.

⸺

TODAY'S MEETING WITH THE prince was big and Rusty was nervous. She stamped out of her mind the picture in Albuquerque of Victor having dinner with a woman on the other side of the dining room. He didn't see her because she and the prince were sitting behind a large planter. But the next morning seeing him try to kiss the same woman was more than she could take. With all the will she could muster, she put those images away in a compartment to be dealt with later.

Rusty had invited her father to join the meeting thinking that his presence might ease the situation of the prince dealing with a woman. Victor was never invited to join the group. Theresa had outdone herself in preparing for the guest. Creamy Lenox china vases had been strategically placed around the house filled with exotic flowers in reds, purples, and oranges spiked with yellow and light-blue gladiolas. The barn employees had scrubbed and scrubbed again the terracotta stone pavers on the barn floor. An Arabic coffee service, the traditional beverage served when guests arrive at a Kuwaiti home, was ready to be served by a wait staff hired for the occasion.

A little before three in the afternoon, a black limo pulled through the ornate gate—arching overhead was the sign: Burns Arabian Horse Ranch. The car continued up the long driveway, circled in front of the house, and stopped. Rusty and her father had been watching for the prince and, at the sight of the limo, walked out onto the long veranda covered by a latticed roof providing shade from the warm sun. Sultan emerged from the vehicle with a spring in his step. He certainly wasn't the stereotypical princely man from the Mediterranean. He was slim, muscular, and wore a white suit, white silk tie and shirt—a handsome man showing his bronze skin, black wavy hair clipped short, and a full, well trimmed, black moustache.

Rusty and her father stepped down the two flagstone risers to greet their visitor.

"Welcome to our ranch, Prince Al Amri. I'd like you to meet my father, Charles Burns." Handshakes, smiles, cordial greetings ensued. Rusty invited the prince into her home. She noticed he hesitated for a moment, looking around at the paddocks in the distance, obviously anxious to see the Arabians she had shown in the ring in Albuquerque. During their dinner at the La Fiesta restaurant he had described to her in great detail how he wanted to build his stables, which was the reason he was looking for especially fine quality Arabians, preferably champions, for breeding purposes. He said he planned to immediately ship the animals to his farm in Kuwait where he would oversee the breeding personally.

"Would you care for a cup of coffee so we can discuss the horses you'll see before going to the barn? It's brewed with your special Arabic coffee bean." She led him to their courtyard—a beautiful interior garden.

"Yes. You are most kind and then we can go to the barn, yes? I'm most anxious to look at the Arabians I saw at the show, to run my hands over their coats. Of course, the pictures you gave me when we shared dinner together were most thoughtful and I studied them carefully."

Shared dinner together. Shared dinner together. Stop remembering that dinner, Rusty thought, instantly visualizing Victor with that woman.

Animated chatter continued between Rusty and the prince, both becoming more and more excited about the prospect of a sale. Rusty believed with all her heart that if she added the prince as a client it would set her up as a bona fide dealer in Arabians. And, on the other hand, she knew the prince had visions of an ever-expanding stable of Arabians as they bred giving him more and more foals—all his friends, and their friends, and then their friends would come to him to buy their Arabs.

"Please, Miss Burns, can we go now to the horses?"

"Certainly, and please call me Rusty." Setting her coffee cup down on the table, she stood, "Dad, will you join us?"

Charles nodded that he would. The three left the courtyard and started down the path. Rusty's father followed a few steps behind his daughter, smiling as they approached the barn. This potential sale was a big step to her goal of becoming famous worldwide. He understood that her chatter had something to do with the fact that her showing the Peterson's stallion had won

Reserve Champion at the show, but would he pass inspection up close by the prince?

Sampson had recovered nicely from the throatlatch surgery. Rusty had given his neck a treatment of Lady Clairol to further mask the alteration and he passed the judges scrutiny with flying colors. The Peterson's had told her if someone wanted to buy the horse they would certainly sell him at a good price. But not a cut-rate figure.

The mare, Moon Beam, was not included in the eight horses Rusty took to the show. She wanted to give her more time, time to allow her eyes to heal completely. She had been led out of the enclosed small barn back on the north side of the ranch a few days ago so her eyes would adjust to the brilliant sunshine.

On the way to the paddocks, Rusty explained to the prince that she was never abusive to the horses under her tutelage. Quite the contrary, they were fed well, given plenty of water, exercised regularly above and beyond their training. What she didn't say was that she had big dreams which meant she had to train and show horses that placed in the top three of every show. She didn't feel that helping the horse along with a little cosmetic surgery was a bad thing. After all, women were getting facelifts all the time, or injections to improve their looks. Rusty had spent many hours grooming the horses she was presenting to the prince.

A stable hand was ready to lead the three mares and Sampson into separate paddocks. Each paddock had a gate into a bigger center ring so Rusty could parade the horse in front of the prince in a large open space.

Sultan became more and more excited as one after the other Rusty paraded the Arabians, saving the best for last—Sampson, the Peterson's stallion.

After seeing what Rusty had to offer again, but now up close, the group returned to the shady courtyard. The wait staff immediately presented a fresh coffee service per Rusty's strict instructions—when they saw her coming, they must pick up the silver trays and enter the courtyard as Rusty and her guest took their seats.

"Would you prefer something besides coffee, something cool to drink?" Rusty asked with a little laugh knowing full well the prince was probably impressed that she had checked to find his favorite coffee. He shook his head, no.

Rusty decided to approach the possible sale of the four Arabs with a positive attitude. She lost her nervousness out in the paddock as the prince had seemed genuinely taken with her selections. "So, Sultan have you decided which of my prized Arabs you wish to add to your farm?"

"Oh, my, yes. I wish I could take them all ... maybe another time, unless, of course, we can come to an understanding. He took a sip of his coffee, then a bite of a flaky biscuit on which he had slathered Theresa's homemade marmalade jam. He leaned back in his chair, eyes closed, saying nothing.

Rusty immediately became alarmed, looking over at her father, raising her eyebrows, questioning what was going on. Sultan sat forward. "Yes, I'll take the stallion ... a fine animal. And, the mare ... the silver-gray with that beautiful, silky black mane and tail. I wish I could buy the two others—the bay and the golden creature. Beautiful, beautiful, all of them."

"Well, take them all. I'm sure we can come to, to an understanding. What's holding you back?" Rusty asked in a sweet, non-threatening voice.

"My brother is going into business with me, you know, to pool our funds. I'm afraid he has not as yet transferred his share. Of course, I'm prepared to make a deposit of two-million dollars and the balance when we receive the horses ... in good condition after such a long journey."

"Well, I had anticipated full payment which is customary when buying my Arabians, but I understand your position ... with your brother being a partner. I think we can go ahead with the whole deal if you increase the deposit to three-million dollars and the balance on a promissory note." Rusty looked at the prince as the adrenaline that was pumping in her body a moment before had turned to anxiety. She was frantic about his offering a deposit, and such a small one. Yet, he was a prince! *A promissory note should be all right. Shouldn't it?*

"You drive a hard bargain, Ms. Burns, Rusty, but I will make the deposit you request and go ahead with the purchase of the three mares and the stallion."

"Good choices. I know you will be pleased. How soon will you be picking them up?"

"I think in the next two days, if that is all right with you, Rusty."

Negotiations for the payment on the note were made, and the deposit paid. The sale was finalized. The prince bid Rusty and her father goodbye. His driver opened the door to the backseat and the prince entered the limo giving a final wave as the car receded down the driveway and out to the highway.

Rusty, her whole body springing with excitement, turned to her father. "I think this calls for a glass of champagne, don't you?" She immediately came down off her high when she saw the look on her father's face. "What's wrong?" she asked sharply, her brows pinching together, lips tightening into a thin line.

"That prince is buying the horses for breeding. I know Victor performed an operation on one of them and also there is something about the tattooing of one of the mare's eyes. You are perpetrating fraud, Rusty. It's not right."

"Dad, the surgery on Sampson was to remove a lump. Fortunately, it was benign. And I don't know where you heard about the eye thing."

"The kid you hired to feed the horses and clean the barns. I saw him coming back a week ago from the little barn on the back of our property, and I asked him if there was a horse back there. He said, yes. That a mare had her eyes worked on so they weren't pink anymore. He also added that she had to stay in the dark until they healed so she wouldn't damage her eyes."

"Oh, that. She had an infection. It's all better now. Come on, Dad don't be such a fussbudget."

"I don't like this path that you've decided to take, Rusty. If you don't change course, I'm afraid you're headed for trouble."

———

THE NEXT DAY RUSTY'S banker drew up the promissory note, ready to be signed when Prince Sultan Al Amri came to pick up the horses.

Chapter 32

___

THERESA SET OUT CRYSTAL flutes for the champagne, some of her special spicy pork nuggets, and crackers with Camembert cheese. She had a smile on her face, believing the meeting was a success since Rusty asked for a special bottle of champagne from the wine cellar. But while Rusty had a big smile on her face, Mr. Burns' face remained stony. She heard Rusty invite Yuma up to the house for a glass of champagne but evidently the Indian had declined. As Theresa set the tray down, Victor joined the group and suddenly Rusty's green eyes were throwing darts his way.

___

SEEING THE CHAMPAGNE, Victor strolled over, ignoring the silence from Rusty and her father. "Okay, you two. This is supposed to be a happy occasion. Let me pop that cork so we can toast the woman of the hour." The cork flew into the air and Victor quickly filled the glasses not letting a drop spill onto the Navajo rug.

After handing out the flutes of champagne, he raised his glass, "Here's to the lady who just put Burns Arabian Horse Ranch on the world map. Rusty you did a helluva job landing the sale for all four horses." Rusty turned her head away from Victor and looked at her dad. He did not join in the toast.

"Excuse me. I have some work to do." Charles said. Setting his champagne on the sideboard he left the room without drinking a drop.

"What's the matter with your dad and you don't look like you're in a celebrating mood either?" Victor said. *Ah, maybe she's mad because she saw me with Elizabeth*, He thought. *She's hardly said a word to me since we left New Mexico.* He sidled over to Rusty giving her a kiss on the cheek in hopes of thawing the ice that seemed to encapsulate her. The kiss didn't find its mark. Rusty jerked away.

She swirled around. "Who was that woman you had dinner with, in Albuquerque?"

So I was right. She did see us. "You'll never believe it," he said.

"Try me."

"She practically accosted me at the ring where I was watching you. You did a terrific job with Sampson by the way. He should have been the champ."

"Don't patronize me, Victor. Who was she?"

"Some lady from Florida turned out she was aware of the Stevens guy. His farm is located in the same town where she lives. So she was asking questions about what was going on in the ring. She came to the show to learn more about Arabians. Seems several of her friends, which didn't include Stevens, have started raising them on their own farms."

"So, how did a few questions end up with dinner?"

"Hey, I was just being polite. You were having dinner with Sultan, which you pointedly didn't invite me to join, so I asked if she would like to have dinner with me. I didn't have time to talk with her at the show, but I could tell her more about the care and grooming, and training of the horses later. I told her I was a vet. We set a time and that was it."

RUSTY WANTED TO BELIEVE HIM. She loved him with every fiber in her body. Maybe he was telling the truth, after all he was a handsome man and she had seen more than one woman throw herself at him. Victor gently put his arms around her. This time she didn't resist and gave in to his passionate embrace.

Leaning back he looked into her eyes, checking to see if her fury had passed. Sensing all was well again between them, he said, "I have an idea, my little firefly, let's take our champagne up to our room and have our own celebration. Besides I have something to give you."

Victor led Rusty, arm around her waist, to their bedroom. Closing the door, he set their glasses down on the small cherry table under the window and then pulled her to him. "Rusty, I love you. Don't ever think there could be another woman." Kissing her forehead, eyes, and then her neck, he slowly undressed her. She did not resist. He thought of nothing but making love to her as he revealed her body, his own body now on fire. He picked her up and laid her on the bed, pulling his shirt off, removing the rest of his clothes, and then gathering her in his arms. She met his passion and, as always in the past when he made love to her, she exceeded his passion sending him into an ecstasy he never thought possible.

They laid entwined, breathing ragged as if they couldn't take another gasp of air. Victor rolled to her side. He felt terrific. He untangled his legs from hers and stood up, taking a few steps to the window to retrieve their champagne.

"I should have brought the bottle along, but we still have a few drops," he said combining the two glasses. With his eyes never leaving her spent body, he dipped his finger in the glass and traced the liquid over her lips.

"I told you I had a gift for you. Don't move—it's here in the drawer. I put it on the bedside table so when the right time came, I could reach for it."

Rusty's head nestled into her pillow, her eyes closed, as the feeling of a woman in love spread through her body. Feeling the touch of velvet on her belly, she slowly opened her eyes, raised herself slightly onto her elbows. A small, black-velvet box was indeed resting on her bare skin.

She looked up at Victor sitting beside her, his arm crossed over her and rested on the bed. "What is this?" she asked.

"Open it and you'll see."

Picking up the little velvet box, she opened the lid. A large solitaire diamond set in white gold sparkled back at her. She looked into Victor's warm eyes and saw his love beaming at her.

"Rusty, will you marry me?"

Tears filled her eyes. She had been waiting for this moment, waiting for him to ask her to be his wife. Maybe this is what he needed, she thought. A commitment from me, to stop wandering around, to stop searching to find a partner. I will be that woman.

"Yes, yes, I'll marry you. I was beginning to think you didn't love me, and now this beautiful ring." She carefully removed the twinkling object from the white satin. "Look, it fits perfectly. How did—"

"I borrowed one of your rings and matched the size. I hope those are tears of joy."

"You know they are." She reached for the knob on the drawer of her bedside table. Sliding it open she pulled out a tissue.

"Rusty, there's a gun in that drawer. How long has that been there?"

"Since I was twelve." She dabbed the tears from her eyes, smiled back at Victor and pulled him down to her to kiss his lips.

Looking up from their ardent embrace, he said, "Why are you keeping a gun?"

"It was a present on my twelfth birthday. Dad taught me how to shoot it, Yuma, too. He felt I should have something to protect myself because we live in a remote area. He and mom have one as well."

"How about protection from your fiancé?" he said with a smile.

Rusty pulled him to her, kissing him with renewed passion. The lovers welcomed the new swell of heat, their bodies responding to each other even more than before.

Spent, Rusty snuggled into Victor's arms. Victor playfully twisted one of her red curls around his finger looking over at the closed drawer.

"Is it loaded?"

"Is what loaded?" she asked dreamily.

"That gun."

Rusty reached for the champagne glass on the bedside table. "Of course, silly. If someone is going to attack me, I can't very well say, 'wait a minute while I put bullets in my gun.'"

Chapter 33

———

THE TRUCK HAULING BLACK Magic's trailer closed the distance to Florida, stopping a few nights along the way. Jerry and Tony took turns driving. However, Tony's turn was always an hour or more longer than Jerry's. Jerry spent most of his time in the passenger seat making calls on his cell phone, or he would pull his hat down over his eyes appearing to be asleep, but in fact he was mulling over the events of the last couple of weeks and what he was going to do about them.

Finally, in the late afternoon, they drove into the farm's driveway, pulling up to the barn. Jerry unloaded Magic and turned him out to the pasture to let him run after being cooped up in the trailer for so many days. Tony went home for some much needed rest.

Barbara heard the truck drive in and ran to the barn to greet her husband. After a brief embrace they walked hand-in-hand into the house. Jerry took a shower and then headed for the kitchen. Barbara, guessing what her husband would do once he got home, had stocked the refrigerator with fresh veggies, and the pantry with jars of stuff including olives, pineapple chunks, a variety of canned beans, as well as several bags of pasta in various shapes.

Sure enough, invigorated by his shower, Barbara found him slicing and dicing on the butcher block—pans were greased and pots of salted water were heating up on the stove. He was mixing up tofu balls with sage and onions. Without saying a word, she went to the garden and harvested several large bunches of fresh basil, chives, and flat-leafed parsley. Returning to the kitchen she put each bunch, one-by-one, into the spinner washing the herbs. She laid them out on paper toweling and then went back to her office.

An hour later, the aroma of eggplant Parmesan, fresh tomato sauce, as well as an Alfredo sauce, drew her back into the kitchen. She kissed Jerry on the cheek, not wanting to disturb the chef in action, and set the kitchen's pine trestle table—two places on one end so she could hear all about the trip but mainly his plan of action.

Jerry looked up to see Barbara lighting the candles on the table, and then uncorking a fine full-bodied Shiraz wine, letting it breathe until the chef was ready to serve the feast. He piled several platters with food and placed them on the table. Sitting down at the head of the table and taking his wife's hand, they bowed their heads and thanked the Lord for their food.

Barbara poured the wine and then picked up her glass, raising it to her husband, "Here's to our Black Magic, and here's to his champion handler. I love you both." The rims of their glasses touched, both enjoying a sip. Jerry leaned over and kissed his wife, giving her a smile that said thanks for understanding.

"Okay, mister, give."

Jerry filled her in on the show—the excitement, the noises, the smells, and the announcement of Black Magic as the champion stallion under halter. Then he got down to business and told her of the telephone conversations he had in route to Florida.

"I first called Linda for her suggestion of another vet who might have the capacity to store frozen semen. She suggested a vet in Leesburg. Turned out he was one of the vets that Liz stopped to see asking if he had seen Desiree."

"Did he have any word on her whereabouts?" Barbara helped herself to the salad of mixed greens, cherry tomatoes, dressed with a light Balsamic vinegar and oil.

"No. Desiree sure has vanished," Jerry said taking the salad bowl Barbara passed to him.

"Linda still thinks we have a chance of recovering her. It won't be long until she's ready to have her foal," Barbara said, sprinkling grated Parmesan on her pasta.

"I pray she's right. Anyway, he was extremely nice and told me all about his facility and equipment. I think we would be safe to use him."

"You know, Liz never liked Wilder. When I told her about the fire, her first words were that he probably set it and kept the straws." Barbara held the basket of soft, golden breadsticks with coarse salt for Jerry, then picked up one for herself.

"Well, as far I'm concerned he's history. Did you have any luck finding an intern or someone with experience in handling semen collections?"

"Yes. Two are coming over tomorrow to meet with you. They are both available so if you like one of them you can hire them on the spot. As for your suggestion to hire an assistant to process the breeding orders, and to follow through with the shipments, I interviewed a young lady yesterday. I liked her very much but I want you to talk to her before we offer her the job. She would also be amenable to taking short-time employment, say two or three months to see how it works out."

"Did Liz call? I saw her a couple of times at the show talking to a man but I don't know who he was."

"Oh, that young lady had quite a day—the day you won. Seems she spotted Rusty Burns in an embrace with a man before she entered the ring with her stallion. So our Liz strikes up a conversation with the man."

"How did she manage to do that?"

"She navigated near him so he bumped into her spilling her coffee. One thing led to another. I'll let her fill you in, but I guess there was one interesting statement he made when they had dinner—"

"Dinner?" Jerry laughed, ladling more sauce onto his eggplant.

"Drinks and dinner. He told her he was a vet but closed his practice to work full time at the Burns' ranch. He said he removed a lump from a horse. He wanted to be sure it wasn't cancerous."

"Oh, sure, not cancerous."

"But wait. He put a move on her."

"A move?"

"Twice. Like in trying to kiss her."

"Wow. Did he succeed?'

"No. But she takes him for a two-timing Romeo. Could be bad news for Miss Burns if she has any romantic ideas."

"More wine, honey?" Jerry asked.

"Yes, please. Detective Milhous called. He had big news. The DNA from the cigarette butt he found in the sink at the intern's mobile home matched with the butt Liz found in the grass by the fence where Desiree went missing. So the two crimes seem to be linked. Again, Liz called it."

Chapter 34

⸻

DAVID AND WHISKEY WERE ABOUT to turn down their driveway when Whiskey suddenly stood her ground. David turned to see what had alerted his friend and saw Liz and Maggie approaching at a good clip.

"Hey, stranger. I haven't seen you since your trip. How was it?" David asked as Liz drew to a halt, Maggie and Whiskey greeted each other enthusiastically, tails wagging.

"Interesting," Liz replied, stooping with her hands on her knees to catch her breath. "I feel like it's been months since my last run—I'm so out of shape."

"How about coming over for dinner tonight? We need to bring each other up-to-date ... on our mutual cases," David said with a grin.

"Sounds great. Can I bring something?"

"Just Maggie. Say about 6:00?"

"We'll be there. Have a good day." Liz flashed him a smile and then she and Maggie jogged off.

"Do you like steak?" David yelled.

"Love it—medium rare."

⸻

DAVID CAUGHT HIS SMILING image in the car window as he fumbled in his pocket for his car keys. Barbara Stevens had called earlier and asked if he would like some eggplant with spaghetti and sauce. Seems Jerry had one of those days when he played chef and cooked up an enormous banquet for two. After stopping at the Stevens farm, he and Whiskey made a quick stop at the supermarket to pick up the steaks.

It took him three trips to the car to unload all the groceries and covered dishes Barbara had given him. He was on his last trip when he caught sight of Liz and Maggie walking down the driveway. Liz looked like a ray of sunshine in yellow slacks, a deep orange long-sleeved shirt, and a purple sweater around her shoulders, knotted in front. Spotting Maggie, Whiskey jumped off the deck that wrapped around the house and they took off chasing squirrels through the forested property.

"Can I help you carry something?" Liz asked laughing at the dogs and the balancing act David was performing with a stack of plastic-covered bowls.

"What's so funny? Here take this dish, if you will, please."

"I'm laughing because I just unloaded some similar bowls at my house. That must have been some meal Jerry put together when he got back from the show. Barbara says he does that when he's making plans, trying to figure something out, or is depressed. She said this was a little more than usual." Liz took the dish from David tucking the bottle of wine she brought for the occasion under her arm.

"I like your outfit—all the colors," David said still juggling the rest of the bowls and the bag of steaks.

"You should have seen me when I was a mail carrier. It was scary, my clothes were so bright. I decided on a complete reversal—mostly black. More professional. Like you, I guess." She smiled up at him. He was wearing his usual black trousers, black short-sleeved T-shirt, but no gun belt.

When they got to the deck, David quickly climbed the steps, put what he was carrying on the small round table and then gave Liz a hand with what she was carrying.

"This is some home you have here, David ... and all that beautiful forest," Liz said turning around for a better look.

Suddenly Whiskey did a flying leap to the deck to join her master. Maggie didn't quite know what to do, pacing back and forth on the grass barking.

"Come on, girl, you can do it," Liz said urging her dog to jump. With her mistress standing above the stairs, Maggie slowly took

BLACK MAGIC | 145

one step at a time and then sat panting next to Liz, her tongue hanging out as she looked up at her mistress with her big brown eyes.

"Let's take all this stuff to the kitchen and then I'll get the steaks going on the barbeque out in the backyard." David led the way through the sliding glass doors. "Watch your step," he cautioned. "This pasta will make a nice side for our steaks. Can you pop it in the microwave?"

"Happy day. Happy day."

"What's that?"

"Polly. The parrot I kindly offered to give you. I'll go start heating up the barbeque."

"Would you like me to put some of these bowls in the freezer before they thaw?"

"Please. I'll be right back." The dogs joined in the fun and this time Maggie, after giving a little whine leaped off following her friend.

Liz found a couple of goblets in the cupboard along with a corkscrew and opened the wine. She poured a little in each glass as David walked in.

"Hey, that looks like what the doctor ordered. Do you want to join me while we cook the steaks?" he said, sprinkling coarse salt and pepper and garlic salt on both sides of the steaks.

"Absolutely. I'll carry our glasses."

It wasn't long before the steaks were sizzling. David opened the door beneath the glowing charcoals retrieving a long fork and a pair of tongs.

"You said medium rare?"

"Yes, I did. How come there are four steaks?"

"I don't know about Maggie, but Whiskey would never forgive me if she wasn't included. Do you think Maggie can handle a steak? Of course, I'll cut it up for her."

"Does a chicken have feathers?"

"Well, okay then. I think they're done so let's get this dinner started."

Whiskey, Maggie right behind her, raced up to David.

"Oh, no. Hold your nose, Liz. Our girls must have found a skunk."

"Oooh, they smell awful," Liz said, her face screwed up as she held her nose. "What are we going to do with them? I've heard tomato juice is good ... absorbs the odor."

"I don't have a tub, but I do have a couple of buckets and a hose. No tomato juice, but there are a few large bottles of Bloody Mary mix in one of the kitchen cabinets."

"Okay, you take the steaks," Liz said, "and I'll try to keep them off the deck and out of the house. Oh, wait. Cut one of the steaks up and I'll entice them to stay on the grass until you get the Bloody Marys."

"Liz, they're not Bloody Marys, they are bottles of a Bloody Mary mix."

Whiskey raced ahead and jumped on the deck.

"No. No, Whiskey. Get down," David yelled.

Whiskey jumped down to the grass just as Maggie pranced up the stairs.

"Maggie, come down," Liz ordered.

Maggie jumped down, but Whiskey followed David back up the stairs.

Liz called the dogs and, showing them what she had in her hand, they rushed up to her, took a morsel and raced back into the woods. David returned, hustling down the steps with four half-gallon bottles of Bloody Mary mix just as Whiskey and Maggie emerged from the woods and ran to their masters. Liz gave them another piece of meat. They obviously thought this was a terrific dog game.

"Here are two bottles for you," David said handing them to Liz. "We'll hose them down, and when they're soaked we can pour the mix over them and rub it in."

The dogs loved the rub down and then it was catch-the-steak game again. Liz threw a piece of the meat in the air, but in her haste to throw it she tripped on the hose. Unable to catch her balance the hose wound around her ankles pointing upward, soaking her from head to toe. Laughing, and pulling her wet hair back out of her eyes, she grabbed the elusive green hose and put a kink in it. David was laughing so hard he almost got entangled with the hose as he tried to help her.

"Turn it off, will you," Liz yelped laughing, still dripping but keeping a tight grip on the folded hose.

"Will do," David said wiping tears from his eyes. "I think that's about all we can do on the odor front. Let's go in and get you some dry clothes and I don't know about you, but I'm starving."

———

DAVID LEANED BACK ON the navy-blue canvas deck chair, sipping the last of his wine. He stole a glance at Liz then turned away. He had loaned her a T-shirt that hit her knees, and a pair of his flannel jogging pants with a draw-string. She rolled the legs up so she wouldn't trip. He had enjoyed her company more than he wanted to admit. "What? What did you say?"

"I was just wondering if anything new had turned up in the case while I was away. I suppose Barbara told you about the fire." Liz asked.

"Yes, she did. As far as the cases are concerned, nothing since we had lunch before your trip. It's getting chilly. Would you like a cup of coffee inside?" David asked.

"That would be nice and then I have to run. My to-do list grew while I was out west."

Liz sat at the kitchen table watching David fix the coffee. "I want to visit Wilder. See if I can learn any more about the fire. I think it's strange that the only loss was Steven's frozen straws," Liz said taking the mug of coffee David handed to her.

"You be careful. I remember you saying you didn't like the guy." David added cream and sugar to his coffee.

"That's right. When you saw Barbara today, did she tell you about the threat to clip Black Magic's tail at the show?"

"Yes, she did. She also said that Rusty Burns' vet, her words were, 'put the make on you.'"

"It was strange ... but, yes he did. I'm not sure why. He may have misinterpreted my interest in the Burns' ranch."

"Sorry, lady. I don't think it was strange. You are a very pretty woman."

"Thank you, kind sir. With that, I think I'll be on my way while I'm ahead." Liz smiled at David and deposited her empty coffee cup in the sink.

"I put your clothes in a bag. It's out on the deck."

Both dogs were stretched out on the grass. David moved in front of Liz offering her his hand as she walked down the three steps carrying the bag with the clothes in her other hand.

Suddenly she fell forward, her heel catching the back of the second step. David caught her and held her to be sure she kept her balance. Neither moved—Liz looked up at David and he looked down into her eyes.

"Thanks ... thanks, I could have fallen on my face." Liz slowly broke away color quickly rising in her cheeks.

Maggie and Whiskey both stood looking to see if they were going to play a new game, but David seemed to have lost his voice.

Liz again said thank you in a soft voice. "Dinner was wonderful."

"Thank you for joining me. Maybe we can do it again sometime," David said as he strolled beside her up the driveway. "Do you want me to drive you home?"

"No, I'm only a little way down the road, besides I have Maggie and she doesn't exactly smell like a rose yet. Besides, I need to walk off all that pasta."

"Oh, yes, the pasta. There's still enough left for an army."

They both laughed, relieved that whatever had happened between them when she fell was over. Or was it?

Chapter 35

———

RUSTY LOVED THE ADVENT of the holidays. Theresa's cooking filled the house with the aromas of her cakes, pies, and cookies she baked for the ranch hands and their families. Some Northerners, however, always became disgruntled—holidays without snow? At least they could pull out their heavy sweaters with the cold desert nights—leaving their galoshes in the trunk.

Rusty sat at her desk watching the shards of light shooting from the diamond on her finger as she playfully moved her hand in the sunlight streaming through the window. It was late afternoon and she was enjoying an early glass of wine. It had been a good day on the ranch. Several potential clients had called inquiring about her grooming and training service. They had either seen her at the Albuquerque show or heard of her by word-of-mouth.

Since Victor had proposed he had been more than attentive—catering to her every request and never turning her ardent advances away. She would awake in the morning and immediately snuggle into his body, playing with the hair on his chest, and entwining her legs with his until they both gave in to the heat her actions stoked. Nighttime proved to be a repeat of their morning. There were many days when she flirted outrageously, tantalizing him into making love to her in the hay, high up in the loft of one of the barns.

Taking another sip of wine, letting the delicate taste roll around on her tongue, she opened her email account. Sultan had sent her a message. *I hope he's telling me the payment has been wired to my account,* she thought.

Reading his message she snapped forward in her chair. "What's this garbage! You want to know if I'll act on your behalf to negotiate for stud service with Stevens stallion, Black Magic?"

She abruptly stood, began pacing around her office.

"The nerve to ask me to contact Stevens," she hissed. "Sultan already has one of the best Arabians on his ranch to say nothing of the fact that I have clients with stallions as good as, if not more perfect than Black Magic. The nerve."

Victor walked into Rusty's office hearing her tirade. She almost ran into him charging from wall to wall.

"Hey, what's the matter?" he asked.

"Take a look at that email on my computer. That's what's the matter," she said in a bitter voice. "After all I've done for him, finding the cream of the crop, and he asks about Black Magic. And, he hasn't even made the payment on the note. And he wants me to arrange a stud deal?"

"You're right, sweetheart. He's in no position to ask you to further extend yourself. Tell him no dice."

"Exactly. Of course, I will phrase it that I have far superior stallions here in the valley if he wants to breed with an Arab other than Sampson. Plus, I'll say my accountant told me that the money has not been deposited yet as per our agreement. But, I'd add that I know he's busy, but I expect it in the next day or two. Stevens! Really. I bet that woman, what's her name, Elizabeth something, put him up to it. I saw him talking to her the day of the show.

—

VICTOR KEPT HIS MOUTH SHUT. He didn't want to remind her that he had had dinner with the woman she was ranting about. *Ah, yes. Elizabeth. Maybe a quick trip east is in order. I could go to Kentucky ... to a conference,"* he thought. *Make a side trip to Florida. I'll dig up her email address tomorrow. I could use a little break.*

Chapter 36

CARRYING THE BAG WITH her wet clothes, Liz strolled home as Maggie darted in and out of the bushes on either side of the road. It was a balmy night for mid-November. She had enjoyed the evening in spite of all the mishaps and was quite taken with David's A-frame house, especially the deck. She added a mental note to her to do list: take Maggie to the doggie shampoo shop in the morning.

Liz flicked on the hall light switch, closing the door behind her. Walking into the kitchen, she dug in her purse for her cell phone, which she had silenced when entering David's driveway earlier. *Luckily I didn't slip it into my pocket—might not have survived my fight with the hose,* she thought.

She was startled to see there were five new messages—all from Stewart Young the Leesburg vet she visited a few months back. She selected the most recent.

"Miss Stitchway, I've been trying to reach you. Please call as soon as you get this message. It's urgent."

Checking her watch, it was only 9:30 so she connected to his number.

"Miss. Stitchway?"

"Yes, sir. This is Elizabeth Stitchway, I'm sorry, I—"

"I think I have the Stevens' mare," he yelled into the phone.

"What? You have Desiree? Did you call Jerry?"

"I've been trying to reach both of you since six o'clock. You're the first to call me back."

"Who brought her in?" Liz asked her voice rising, matching Young's excitement.

"A guy. Big guy. He said he had a mare he wanted me to check. He wondered if I could tell when she might foal."

"Is she okay?"

"Appears to be. I checked her over while waiting for you or Mr. Stevens to call me back."

"I presume the man left. Did he say when he would be back?"

"Oh, yea. He wanted me to check her right then and there, but I stalled and told him to come back tomorrow. He wanted to know when I'd be here. Didn't care if I was open or not."

"What did you tell him?"

"7:00 o'clock. Actually, I'm here by six but I didn't let him know that."

"Mr. Young, if you don't mind I'd like to drive down now to see her. I figure it will take less than an hour which would make it close to 10:30—give or take. Is that okay?"

"Yes, sure. I've left several messages—hang on, I've got an incoming call."

Waiting for the vet to come back on the line, Liz refreshed Maggie's water bowl, pulled two bottles of cold water out of the fridge along with a pack of Oreo cookies from the cabinet. She put the supplies in her backpack and hustled to the bedroom to change into her own clothes, dropping David's into the clothes hamper.

"Miss. Stitchway, that was Mr. Stevens. I told him you were driving down and he wants to come with you. He'll certainly be able to identify his mare."

"Okay, I'm out the door. I'll call Jerry."

"Wait. Drive up to the side of my clinic and flash your headlights a couple of times. I'll open the gate."

"Gotcha. Bye." Liz snatched her keys off the counter and threw her backpack over her shoulder. "Sorry, Maggie girl. You can't come with me. You still smell bad. Go get your pillow—I'll be back in a few hours."

Liz pulled out of her driveway at the same time punching Jerry's code on her cell."

"Liz, I'm coming with you," he shouted into the phone.

"I was sure you would. I'm on the road and will pick you up in about five." Liz clicked off and immediately selected David's number.

"David, it's Liz. Hope I didn't get you up."

"No, no, Whiskey and I are outside—trying to air her out before going indoors. She's sleeping in the kitchen tonight. We enjoyed your visit."

"Me, too, but I have some information. I'm on my way over to the Stevens' farm to pick up Jerry."

"What's going on?"

"We had a call from the Leesburg vet, Stewart Young, you know I told you I stopped there awhile ago looking for anything I could find on Desiree. He's pretty sure he has Jerry's mare."

"How did he get her?"

"He said a man dropped her off about 5:30 today. The man said he'd come back around seven in the morning to pick her up. If he's the guy, do you have jurisdiction to arrest him?"

"I'll set it up. Call me after Jerry confirms it's Desiree. Call me either way."

———

AT 10:55 LIZ TURNED OFF the road onto the vet's gravel driveway. She flashed her headlights as instructed and the gate slowly swung open. She drove to the end of the building where Young was standing to meet them and signaled where to park. The gate swung shut behind her car.

"Mr. Stevens, it's good to see you." Young, extending his hand, walked over to Jerry as he climbed out of the car. Liz walked around the other side of the car and Young, hustling around the car to her, gripped her hand vigorously. "Good to see you again, too, Miss Stitchway."

"Liz, please. Enough with the Stitchway," she said smiling.

"And make it Jerry."

Turning back to Jerry, Young said, "I received your second shipment of frozen straws yesterday."

"Barbara told me you had confirmed they arrived safely. Stewart, can we look at the mare?"

"Oh, yes, here I'm blathering away. Come on, she's in here." Young led Jerry and Liz in through the back end of the barn which in turn connected to the clinic.

"She's up in the front stall, on the right."

"Jerry jogged ahead, calling to Desiree. The mare whinnied in reply and stuck her nose up against the bars on the stall's door.

"My pretty girl, it is you." Jerry opened the stall and stepped inside. The mare nuzzled his sleeve as he drew a carrot from his pants pocket. He was ready with a treat, hoping the horse would be Desiree.

While Jerry was stroking the mare and looking her over, Liz called David.

"Hi, it is Desiree. You should see—"

"Hold on, you're talking too fast miss PI. Jerry's sure?"

"Absolutely, you should see the two of them."

"Okay. Are you coming back to Ocala?"

"No, we're staying here. I talked with Dr. Young while we were driving here, you know, to make plans if he did have Desiree. He lives on the property and said there were plenty of bedrooms for Jerry and me. I'm sure I won't sleep, though. I'm going to keep an eye on the entrance in case the man comes early or tries something. The name the man gave was Bernie Wilder but his description wasn't anything like Harold Wilder in Jacksonville ... could be his son I guess."

"How about the horse trailer. Did the vet give you a description?"

"Yes. Young said the man was driving a beat-up, black Dodge truck. The two-horse trailer was a dirty white, no writing on either the truck or the trailer." Liz stuffed her notepad back into her jacket pocket.

"I've talked to the Leesburg PD. We'll stake out the road leading to the clinic. When the guy drives in we'll pull up behind and block him after he enters the building."

"Okay, be careful."

"You be careful," David said. "No heroics."

Chapter 37

—

AT 6:35 A.M. THE NEXT morning a black pickup truck, hauling a dingy white horse trailer, drew up to the side gate of the Young Equine Medical Center in Leesburg. The sky was a light gray—another thirty minutes and the sun would be peeking over the horizon.

A large man in jeans, black leather jacket, cowboy boots and hat emerged from the driver's side of the truck. He sauntered to the front entrance and tried the door. It was locked. He walked back to his truck and pulled out a pack of cigarettes from his shirt pocket. Shaking one loose, he lit up and leaned back on the truck door crossing his legs and exhaled.

Young was inside peeking out the drawn shades of the front window. The lights were out. Liz was in Young's house about twenty-five yards away. She couldn't see the entrance but she did see the man light the cigarette. She called David's cell.

"He's here—out front and—"

"Yea, we saw the truck go by," David broke in.

"David, he's smoking. We have to get that cigarette. If tests match it with the DNA of the other two we found, this guy is history."

"I agree." David said "Let me know when Young opens the door. We'll move in and block the truck."

"Young is going to open the gate and direct the man to drive in with the trailer supposedly to load Desiree. When he clears the gate Young will close it. He'll have the guy come in the back of the barn so you can come in the front. Maybe one of you should stay by the gate just in case. What's the Leesburg's officer's name?"

"Liz, I think we can handle it. His name is Ben."

"Are you in uniform?"

"No, plain clothes. Ben's in uniform and driving a black and white. I'm in a dark blue sedan. We don't want to spook him into doing something stupid like pulling out his taser."

"Is Whiskey with you?"

"You've got to be kidding—no riding in the car with that smell."

"Ditto with Maggie."

———

6:59 A.M. THE SUN CLEARED the horizon. The man flicked his cigarette butt into some bushes next to the building and charged up to the entrance. He tried the doorknob without success, pushed the doorbell three times, and then banged on the door.

"Hey, you must be in there. Open up. I ain't got all day," he hollered.

"I'm coming. I'm coming. Keep your shirt on." Young unlocked the door and the man charged inside.

"Took you long enough. I want my horse. Now."

"Let's settle up then I'll open the gate so you can drive in. There's plenty of room to turn around in the yard. I'll open the barn door so you can load your horse."

"How much? Remember I only asked you to take a look at her."

"That's all I did, plus checked to see that the foal's vitals were good. That's $200."

"You've got to be kidding, $200 just to pat her down?"

"There's more to it than that."

"Shit. Here, put it on my card."

Completing the transaction, which included the signature of Bernie Wilder, Young pushed the button to open the gate and told Wilder he'd meet him out back.

———

LIZ WATCHED THE MAN climb into his truck. The gate swung open; the truck and trailer rolled through as the gate swung shut.

"DAVID, THE GUY DROVE IN THE GATE. YOUNG IS STANDING AT THE BACK, OUTSIDE. THE TRUCK IS TURNING AROUND. IT STOPPED. HE'S OUT OF THE TRUCK ... HE'S OPENING THE BACK OF THE TRAILER."

"WE'RE ON OUR WAY. IS THE GATE SHUT?"

"YES."

———

DAVID DROVE ONTO THE gravel driveway, tires crunching the stone, and parked facing the front entrance. Ben, following in his black and white, stopped facing the gate, the car's bumper almost touching. He climbed out and crept behind the bushes to the left of the gate.

Entering the building David walked straight through the reception area, on through the examination room, and opened the door into the barn as Young and the man entered from the back. The man looked up at David striding fast toward him.

"Oh, no you don't," Wilder yelled. "You ain't taking me." He turned and ran to his truck. The keys were hanging out of the ignition. He started the engine jamming the shift into gear and floored the gas pedal. The truck and trailer lurched forward. Picking up speed Wilder looked up and saw the closed gate and the squad car. It was too late. The truck and trailer crashed through the gate, smashing into the black and white. With the force of the impact and the trailer crashing in behind the truck, Wilder shot forward into the windshield.

Ben called for the emergency medical team as David sprinted to the gate, forced his way between the truck and the torn fence to the driver's side of the truck. The door was jammed. He could see Wilder lying against the steering wheel, blood streaming down his cheek.

"Can you get the other door open?" David called to Ben.

"Got it," Ben yelled back crawling in to see if the man had a pulse.

Sirens in the distance soon closed in, the medical van squealing into the driveway. The van came to a halt and the EMTs scrambled out. They quickly extricated Wilder and whisked him away to the local hospital's emergency center.

No sooner had the EMT van departed when Barbara drove in with a horse trailer attached to the back of her truck. She navigated around the vehicles, pulling to a stop at the edge of the circular driveway.

Liz and Jerry had run out of Young's house to the barn when they saw the truck and trailer tear through the gate. They both entered the clinic through the back of the barn and on out the front door. Barbara climbed out of the truck into Jerry's arms. He gave her a bear hug then grabbed her hand and pulled her into the clinic to see Desiree. This year Thanksgiving was going to be especially meaningful for the Stevens.

Liz, following Jerry out the front of the clinic veered to her left as Jerry veered right to Barbara. Thinking about the scene later, Liz was not sure why she ran up to David, threw her arms around him and gave him a hug.

"Are you all right?" she asked backing away, flustered, cheeks burning.

"Sure am, but that was some sight—that truck, then the trailer, and the noise."

"Hey, David," Ben called out, stuffing his cell in his pocket. "One of the medics just called. The guy came to as they entered the hospital. When one of my officers walked up to him, read him his rights, and told him he was under arrest for stealing a horse and under suspicion for murder, he started yelling that he was innocent and that it was all his old man's idea."

"Oh, wait a minute," Liz said. She walked over to the bushes next to the clinic, pulling branches to the side, stepping in a little further, backing out, and in again. She stooped down, disappearing from sight. Struggling to retrieve her notepad, she tore out a sheet of paper, pinched the paper together, and picked up an object. Shielding her hand, she emerged from the bushes with a triumphant look on her face.

"Detective David Milhous, I bet with this little butt you can replace the word suspicion with a charge of murder."

Chapter 38

———

ELEVEN O'CLOCK THURSDAY MORNING, the week following Thanksgiving, Rusty was running late for her appointment. A lady had called the day before, asking the trainer to evaluate her unruly yearling. Rusty snapped up her hairbrush sweeping it through her tousled hair, trying to smooth it down. With a swipe of wild-berry lipstick and a spritz of perfume, she was ready to go.

Walking to the kitchen she reversed direction hearing the ring of the front doorbell. Passing the window which faced the driveway, she saw a black sedan parked in front of the house. The doorbell rang again just as she pulled it open. A man in a black business suit, black tie, and white shirt, quickly pulled his hand back from the bell.

"Hello. I'm looking for Rebecca Burns."

"Well, you're in luck. I'm Rebecca Burns."

"Here, ma'am. This is for you. Have a nice day." The man handed Rusty an envelope, turned around, and headed back to his car.

Closing the door, Rusty looked at the large, document-sized envelope with the return address of the Arizona State Court House in the upper left corner. The envelope was addressed to Miss Rebecca Burns with her address below.

She tried to pull up the flap but the adhesive stuck fast. In the kitchen, she removed a knife from the oak block. Laying the package on the counter she slit the envelope open. Rusty removed a half-inch thick document and read the cover letter.

Slamming the sheaf of papers down on the counter, she called Victor from the kitchen phone. Hearing him pick up, she yelled, "The bastard is suing me."

"Rusty, stop yelling. I can't understand you."

"I said the bastard is suing me," she repeated emphasizing each word. Seething, she charged from one side of the kitchen to the other, pressing the cordless phone to her ear.

"Does this bastard have a name?" Victor asked.

"Sultan! It seems he had a vet look at the horses we shipped. The stupid vet told him that Moon Beam's eyes had been altered and that Sampson's throat had been cut, as well his ears trimmed. He's suing me for fraud, misrepresentation of the horses, and damages."

"Damn."

"Is that all you've got to say? I'm ordered to appear in court to answer these complaints a week from Friday, at ... at 10:30 in the morning and your response is *damn*."

"How much is he suing you for?"

"Oh, just a measly little old twenty-million dollars."

Victor's whistle pierced her ear. "What are you going to do?" he asked.

"It's not what am I going to do. It's what are we going to do, mister?"

Chapter 39

———

LIZ WAS POUNDING THE pavement on her morning jog when Maggie suddenly spun around and barked. David and Whiskey quickly closed the gap between the pair. Four abreast they continued on down the road.

"How about lunch today?" David asked. "It's supposed to be nice so I could pick up a couple of burgers and meet you at the park with the dogs that is if you're not working on a Saturday."

"The park in December—love to," Liz replied. "I heard a couple of things on the radio regarding Wilder I'd like to ask you about. Where were you thinking? What time?"

"How about Tuscawilla Park, say 1:30. I'll bring lunch. Do you know where the park is?"

"Yes, it's not far from my office. I take Maggie there once in awhile for a quick outing. Sounds terrific. See you there—in the parking lot. If something comes up we can call each other." Liz and Maggie peeled off heading home.

———

THE SUN WAS WARM but the air had turned to a cool sixty-five degrees. David in jeans and a black long-sleeved T-shirt was sitting on a bench with Whiskey standing beside him when Maggie trotted up to her friend. The two danced around each other, touching noses, tails wagging and generally tying up their owners with their leashes. Liz and David laughed as they untangled the leather straps.

Spotting a picnic table under a large, moss-laden live oak, David gave a nod to Liz. "How about we eat over there? You take the girls and I'll grab the cooler out of my car."

"Do you need some help?" Liz asked grasping Whiskey's leash.

"Nope. You go relax ... enjoy your day off, if there is such a thing in our business."

David returned with a small cooler, enough for a couple of beers and a large brown paper bag. "I don't know about you, but I'm starving. Hope you like Reubens," he said pulling out several packets of food, individually wrapped.

"One of my favorites."

"Here are a couple of raw-hide bones for the dogs, and hushpuppies for you and some for me." David dug into the bag again retrieving napkins, mustard, and two dill pickles. "Now the beer and we can dive in." He twisted off the cap, handing the beer to Liz, then did the same for himself.

"This is perfect. Thanks for suggesting it. You didn't tell me we were going gourmet." Taking a sip of her beer, Liz looked over to David. "Last night on the news, the reporter said that Wilder Jr. admitted to tasing, in his words, 'the kid at the equine center.' But he swore it was an accident. The reporter read the statement from his arraignment indicating his father, the vet I met in Jacksonville, was trying to finagle some of Black Magic's semen without paying the breeding fee."

David took a bite of his sandwich. "Remember, this was before Stevens contacted him about a business deal to store the straws. According to the son, his father couldn't believe his good luck when Stevens visited to check out his facility, but, of course, the intern was now dead and Desiree was stolen. If they hadn't been in such a hurry, they would have had what they wanted without the rest of the troubles. But then Stevens would have had a different problem and one that would have been harder to detect—a few missing straws here and there."

"Right, but long before that Wilder was aware that Linda had sole storage of the straws, and he thought his son could get 'the kid' to give him a few if he paid him a couple hundred dollars." Liz popped a hushpuppy into her mouth, closed her eyes relishing the cornmeal treat. Opening her eyes, she continued, "Bernie Wilder admitted he had struck up a friendship with Rick. They then became crack buddies so to speak. That night he visited Rick, they smoked some pot but good old Bernie made a mistake by throwing his cigarette butt in the sink where you found it the next day. So it seems Rick was cooperating with Bernie. But something happened to spook Rick—"

"My guess is he got cold feet once they were in the equine examination room." David squirted some mustard on his sandwich.

"Remember, Linda told us she heard a horse whinny in the early morning hours. Animals know, don't they, when something isn't right. Maggie is up at the window at least once during the night." Liz looked at the dogs. They were laying side-by-side, bones between their paws, shifting their heads when somebody walked down the path to a footbridge spanning the narrow creek.

"According to his statement, Bernie said Rick threatened to come clean with Linda and that's when he tased him. Never in a million years did he think it would kill the kid. In fact, when he left he thought Rick was just knocked out. It wasn't until the news report that an intern had died suddenly at the equine center that he realized what he'd done."

"Do you think he'll get off easy?" Liz asked, taking a swallow of beer.

"Oh, he's definitely looking at jail time."

"The reporter never said why he stole the mare." Liz said, finishing her beer.

"She didn't read the whole statement. He put all the blame on his dad. Rick told Bernie that Desiree was having Black Magic's foal. Bernie figured that was another way that they would get at least a bloodline from Black Magic. He stopped by the Stevens barn one day when he saw Jerry and Barbara leave. He talked to a worker and found out which mare was Desiree. He said he drove up that dirt road several nights until he finally spotted Desiree in that back pasture."

"And, I found the second cigarette butt."

"Liz, the two butts you found, along with the one I found in Rick's sink, really nailed Bernie. They put him at all three places—

tied him up in a neat little bow." David leaned over to make sure the dogs were behaving.

"I sure didn't like Harold Wilder," Liz said. "Not one bit. And, then, of course, they still had Desiree."

"Strange how threads come together. I'm not sure Young would have called about the mare but for your stopping and talking to him that day, leaving more posters of Desiree. She was truly on his radar screen."

"It was lucky Bernie picked Young's clinic. He said he didn't dare take her to his father's—too close for comfort, I guess." Liz gathered up their trash and threw it in the barrel a few feet away while David put the empty beer bottles back in the cooler.

"Want to take the dogs for a walk?"

"Thought you'd never ask," Liz replied a smile spreading across her face.

"Just let me run put this cooler in the car."

Maggie and Whiskey immediately got to their feet, tails wagging, tongues hanging out in anticipation. The bones were long gone.

David returned, untied them and handed Maggie's leash to Liz. They strolled along several paths, Maggie and Whiskey politely trotting alongside. They came to a bench overlooking the narrow stream with three ducks enjoying the water. The dogs stood at attention. David and Liz settled on the bench and with a sharp command the dogs laid down at their feet but kept their eyes on the ducks.

Liz dug in her jacket's side pocket and retrieved two nips. "Would you care for a little Jack Daniels No. 7?" she asked, handing it to him and beaming at the surprised look on his face. Liz opened a nip of Chardonnay for herself.

"I was just thinking it would be nice to have a drink on such a beautiful afternoon, after all it is cocktail time somewhere," David said with a little laugh. "Thanks, Stitch."

Liz handed him the little bottle. She had an odd look on her face.

"What? What did I say?" David asked, unscrewing the tiny cap.

"You're the second man to call me that."

"Should I be jealous?" David asked with a smile.

Liz wasn't sure what surprised her more, the fact he called her Stitch or that he asked if he should be jealous.

"No, no. In fact I'm sure you've met him or know of him. Joe Rocket, the man who was my first real client."

"Oh, yes, the financial management guy working for Stevens."

Suddenly the sprinklers came on shooting water over the grass, over the bench, and on David and Liz. David grabbed Liz's hand pulling her out of range of the spray, and the dogs with her. Whiskey and Maggie, ready for the new game, shook themselves. David and Liz, laughing, reined in the dogs.

"I think we'd better walk some more. Try to dry off," Liz said still laughing.

A family sitting on the other side of the stream witnessed the melee, then the couple walking hand-in-hand with their dogs down the path away from the sprinklers.

Chapter 40

RUSTY SLAPPED THE STEERING wheel of her truck traveling twenty-miles-per-hour over the speed limit—she didn't notice and didn't care—her long red hair shooting out in flaming streaks from the open window.

"That lawyer of mine is worthless. Worthless!" she screamed at the cactus flying by her window. Fumbling for her cell in the pocket of her handbag, she pounded in his code, her hand shaking as she held the device to her ear. She heard him pick up, "Stan, you did nothing for me in court today. Thanks for *nothing* you fool. You're fired!" she screamed, then smacked the top down disconnecting the call. "And you, Victor," she shrieked. "Giving a deposition. You never mentioned that little fact to me. Telling the damn lawyers I ordered you to do the surgeries. What did you think you were doing? Saving your sorry ass? Well, if I go down, you're going with me," she yelled at the driver of a passing semi-truck.

"Twenty-million dollars? Jail time for fraud? Not me, buster."

Pulling through her ranch's gate she swerved to a stop in front of the house. Dust clouds continuing to eddy along the driveway from the speed of the truck. Storming in the front door, she marched into her father's study.

Charles and Henry were sitting in their easy chairs having tea when the door burst open. Rusty, black spiked heels boring into the floor, black silk suit, white blouse open several buttons revealing her ample cleavage, an outfit she carefully picked out to overwhelm the judge now in disarray, stood before her parents. The fire in her eyes matched her wind-swept hair. She slapped the truck's keys down on the console table by the door. A bouquet of flowers teetered then crashed to the floor.

"Well, aren't you going to say something? Something like, 'how did it go in court today, dear?'"

Henry looked from her daughter to her husband. She'd never known how to handle Rusty's outbursts so she certainly wasn't going to get in the middle of this one.

"I take it your appearance in court didn't go well," Charles said in a low controlled voice. Electricity filled the room. No one moved. Their eyes riveted on their daughter.

"Why didn't you tell me you gave a deposition, *father*?" Her question dripping with sarcasm.

"I was well aware you would find out sooner or later. For the sake of peace in the house, even if for only a week, I chose the latter." Charles sighed and gently set his teacup down on the gleaming oak table in front of him. Reaching over he took hold of Henry's hand. "I've told you right along, Rusty, that I didn't approve of the operations you asked Victor to perform on the horses."

"Interesting choice of words—operations *I* asked Victor to perform. I don't suppose you'd believe me if I told you Victor was the one who suggested them."

"It's your ranch. You're in charge. It was only a matter of time until someone was going to call you on it."

Henry gripped her husband's hand as he spoke. Her knuckles white, breathing so shallow she seemed to have turned to stone.

"And Yuma," Rusty spit out the Navajo's name. "Who told Sultan's attorney to talk to him?"

"I did," Charles said.

"Did you know about the pictures?"

"Yes," Charles said softly.

"Have you seen them?"

"Yes."

"Nice shots. Very clear. Painfully clear. How could you turn against me?"

"Rusty, you need help," Charles said, pain filling his eyes. "You've changed. You're not my little firecracker anymore. Not the little girl who slept outside Patty's stall so the pony could rest before a show. You lost yourself somewhere along the way."

"Your father and I will stand by you," Henry said, her voice barely a whisper. "We've contacted a doctor."

"Stand by me? This is what you call standing by me? Testifying against me and saying I need a shrink?" Rusty stood by the door. Her body so tight that if anyone or anything touched her she would shatter. "If this is standing by me, please don't bother. Where the hell is Victor?"

"He's waiting for you in your office," Charles said.

Rusty snatched her keys from the table, turned on her heel, and left her parents. Her spike heels clicked on the tile floor as she charged down the hallway to her office. Victor wasn't there when she entered the room, however, his computer was running. It appeared he had been interrupted checking his email. Rusty passed his desk and wouldn't have stopped except she caught the name of the addressee. Elizabeth Standish. Rusty bent down to read the message Victor had just sent. The first sentence was all she needed: "I'm coming to Florida next week. How about dinner? I've missed seeing you."

Rusty burst from the room and ran up the stairs to their bedroom. Victor was sitting on the edge of the bed talking on his cell phone.

Rusty walked to her nightstand and jerked open the drawer. She picked up the gun, turned to face Victor who had closed his cell and shifted to face her just as she pulled the trigger ... and pulled it again.

"Rusty, I—" He slumped forward on the bed then slid off clutching the satin spread, pulling it to the floor with him.

Rusty threw the gun on the bed and ran down the stairs, heels again clicking on the tile floor. She yanked the front door open and darted out to her truck. She sped down the driveway, plumes of dust billowing up in the wake of the speeding truck.

Chapter 41

ON FRIDAY THE THIRTEENTH of December, at 5:41 in the afternoon, a 9-1-1 call was placed from the Burns' ranch. The caller said a man had been shot, was losing blood, and appeared to be unconscious.

When the medics arrived, followed immediately by the police, Charles and Henrietta Burns met them at the front door. Henry stood to one side of the door wide-eyed, immobilized with shock, as the group rushed by. Charles Burns escorted the group, including the two police officers to Rusty and Victor's bedroom.

The EMTs knelt beside Victor, applying compresses trying to stem the bleeding. Then they whisked him off to a waiting medical chopper, and on to a trauma center in Phoenix.

The police officers surveyed the crime scene. One detective, who had taken pictures of Victor before the medics moved him, continued to photograph the room.

Charles stood in the doorway, watching, grim-faced, hands clenched, trying to hold himself together. The other officer turned to Charles.

"Can we go downstairs? I have to ask you and your wife some questions."

"Yes, Officer. Follow me. I'll get my wife."

Entering the living room, Henry sat down on the couch, the officer sat in a chair facing her across a coffee table. Charles poured a large shot of whiskey into a highball glass at the mini-bar. He did not sit down. He turned from the bar and stood facing the officer.

"My name is Detective Williams. For the record will you give me your names please?"

"I'm Charles Burns and this is my wife, Henrietta Burns," Charles said, taking a long swallow of his drink.

"Is that your name, ma'am? Henrietta Burns?"

Henry nodded, pulling on the hanky in her hand. Her face drawn and pale as white ice.

"And the injured man?"

"Victor Bennett," Charles said.

"Thank you," the detective said, writing on his small notepad. He looked up at the couple. "What happened here, folks?"

"I shot the bastard," Charles said. His voice was strong but not elevated.

Henry jumped up. "Charles, you did not. Don't say such a thing. Stop trying to protect her. She's on her own now. You can't baby her any longer."

"Excuse me," the detective interrupted. "Who is the she you are referring to?"

"Rusty, our daughter," Henry said looking wildly back and forth from Charles to the detective and back to Charles. "Charles, you couldn't have done it. We were together in your study."

"If you recall, Henry, I left the room right before Rusty stormed out of the house. You wandered in later, calling me, wondering where I was."

"Well ... I don't remember ... I guess you did ... leave the room."

"Mrs. Burns, if you say your husband didn't shoot Mr. Bennett, who did?"

"Our daughter, Rusty. She's been under a lot of strain and today ... the court appearance ... must have pushed her over the edge. I told her she needed to see a doctor. Charles told her she had changed, that she needed help. Didn't you Charles?" Henry said pleading to her husband to agree with her.

"Who last saw Mr. Bennett?"

"Rusty—" Henry said.

"I did." Charles cut in.

"Where is this Rusty?"

"She left the house," Henry and Charles said in unison.

Henry broke into tears, covering her face with her handkerchief. Charles downed the rest of his drink and walked back to the bar to pour another.

"Do either of you know where she went?"

"No. She didn't say where she was going," Charles said. Moving to the back of the couch he patted Henry's shoulder, but she continued to sob, her body racking in sorrow.

"Mr. Burns, if you shot Mr. Bennett, where is the gun?"

"On my desk ... in my office."

Chapter 42

———

RUSTY PULLED INTO THE parking lot of her bank. Inside, she sauntered up to her favorite teller and filled out a withdrawal slip for $100,000. It was not quite six o'clock.

"Hi, Alice. Need some money to buy a horse."

"Must be a winner for this kind of dough." Alice flashed a smile and laughed as she counted out twenty $5,000 bills. She didn't seem fazed by the amount. Rusty had withdrawn large sums of money before.

Stuffing the bills into a zippered compartment of her handbag, Rusty strolled out of the bank. Once again on the road, she stomped on the gas pedal. The truck responded, flying south on I-17. Grasping her cell phone lying in the cup tray of the console, she flipped to the page with stored telephone numbers and selected the Glendale Municipal Airport.

"Is Eddy there? Please get him for me. Tell him it's Rusty."

Gripping the steering wheel, foot clamped to the gas pedal, phone to her ear, her mind was formulating a plan to get even with Elizabeth Standish. Then she thought about Black Magic and Stevens, Maybe she'd throw him into the mix for good measure.

"Hi, Rusty. What can I do for you?" a man said, his voice interrupting her thoughts.

"Hi, Eddy. By any chance is that Cessna I like available for a couple of days?"

"She sure is. When would you like it?"

"Actually, I'm on my way to your airport now. Could you gas her up?"

"Will do. Where ya going?"

"Las Vegas. Friends of mine are giving a party. Will a tank take me over and back?"

"Hell, yes. That baby has a range of 1600 miles."

"Perfect. See you in about forty minutes, and Eddy, as usual, this is just between you and me. Someday I'll surprise my folks with a trip to San Francisco, but not yet."

Rusty disconnected the call, then jerked open the glove compartment. She removed a gun she always kept there for protection when she was on the road and stuffed it into her handbag.

Chapter 43

"JERRY! JERRY!" BARBARA SCREAMED running from the barn.

Jerry was working in his study trying to come up with a faster way to ship the straws when he heard Barbara's screams. He immediately ran to the front door.

"What's the matter? What's happened?"

"Black Magic. *He's down.* Hurry."

Jerry darted past her and ran as fast as he could, not daring to breathe, fear gripping his body. Entering the barn, he ran to Magic's stall. The stallion was on his back, laying in such a way that he was unable to return to his feet. He had cast himself against the wall. Jerry stroked his neck but when he tried to help the horse to a position where he could set his feet to rise, the horse cried out in pain. "Call Linda," he yelled. "Tell her it's an emergency."

"I did, the minute I saw him. I knew it was bad. She's on her way. Oh, Jerry, is he going to be okay?"

"I don't know. He's in awful pain." Jerry glanced around the stall. There were no signs of the horse struggling to free himself. The hay was strewn about but that wasn't unusual. Black Magic liked to roll in the hay, wriggling around on his back. But this time he couldn't right himself. He had just laid there waiting for his human friends to help him.

"The stress of laying in this position could have caused a twist in his gut. Oh, God," Jerry prayed kneeling beside his horse. "Please don't let his stomach rupture. Don't let him die. Please, please don't let him die." Jerry continued to stroke Black Magic's neck.

They heard Linda's truck skid to a stop outside the barn—the truck door slammed. She came running into the barn with her medical bag, immediately kneeling by the stricken horse. Linda gently touched his side. He cried out in pain. Digging in her bag, she quickly pulled out a syringe, prepared the needle and gave him a shot. "Hopefully this will relieve some of his pain." She scanned his body for clues as to the origin of his distress. She glanced around the stall, as Jerry had done minutes before. The stall was neat. Looking back to the stricken horse she saw no scratches or cuts from the horse rolling or thrashing.

Jerry continued to stroke his friend's neck, tenderly touching his forelock. "I was too late. I wasn't here when you needed me." Tears now streamed down Jerry's face. Barbara, kneeling behind her husband, put her hand on his shoulder, and then bent her head down on his back her tears flowing onto Jerry's shirt.

Linda continued to administer drugs to the stallion but nothing seemed to work. Her eyes filled with tears. She looked up at Jerry. "The drugs eased his pain but they aren't helping him move from his position. I think his stomach ruptured apparently from a colic that happened during the night."

Suddenly, Black Magic lifted his head and with a great effort slowly rose to his feet. Jerry, Barbara and Linda rose with him, gently caressing his coat. Maybe. Maybe. Magic looked into Jerry's eyes as if to say goodbye and then collapsed to the floor of his stall.

The barn fell silent.

The three who were with him when he entered this world looked down in disbelief. Their beloved friend had left them.

Chapter 44

———

IT WAS AFTER MIDNIGHT Sunday morning when Rusty landed her plane in Baton Rouge, Louisiana, some 1400 miles from Glendale, Arizona. Her adrenaline was spent and all she could think of was a warm shower and a soft pillow. Renting a car from a sleepy-eyed agent, she drove out of the airport and merged onto I-10. She stopped at the first motel she saw.

Slapping the counter bell several times, a door opened from the back and a man shuffled up to the counter in his robe and slippers. He shoved a registration slip in front of her and gave her a pen. She handed him a hundred-dollar bill and he gave her a few dollars in change. He handed her the key to room 27. Neither one spoke. She picked up the key and went to her room.

Collapsing on the bed, the shower forgotten, she fell into a deep sleep until she heard the hum of a vacuum in the next room. Opening her eyes, disoriented for a moment, her head snapped up off the pillow. She was immediately in the same frame of mind that had driven her to shoot Victor. Elizabeth Standish. The woman who had enticed Victor, stealing him away, dealing a death blow to Rusty's way of life and her future dreams.

Rusty retrieved her laptop from the car. Back in the room, she started up the computer and entered the internet. She began her search for Standish by looking up the Stevens Arabian Horse Farm. She thought he lived in Ocala but wasn't sure. Victor had said Standish and Stevens knew each other.

Stevens' farm popped up immediately. She wrote down the address and phone number. Nothing came up for the name of Standish. Grabbing her cell phone from the bedside table, she called information. The operator couldn't find a Standish either— not in Ocala or any of the surrounding areas.

Furious she could not locate the woman, Rusty showered, then dressing in the clothes she fled in, she left the motel. Her destination: Ocala. She drove a couple of miles and pulled into a Denny's. Ordering a breakfast sandwich to go, she picked up a Florida map and asked where she might buy a pair of jeans. The fresh-faced cashier told her there was a general store, east two blocks, on her right. She couldn't miss it.

An hour later, and another cup of coffee in the car's beverage tray, the small store was left behind, less two pairs of jeans, a pair of boots, a belt, a leather shoulder bag and four shirts. She transferred the contents of her handbag, including the gun, to the new roomier tote. After her shopping spree, she traced her route on the map from Baton Rouge to Ocala. From all indications, following the I-10 highway into Florida, and then onto I-75, she figured she could make it in a day, a day and a half at most.

Contemplating the length of time to Florida, Stevens jumped back in her thoughts. Her brain switched alternately between plans to get Standish and punishing Stevens. She had heard whispers that Stevens felt she was doing something morally wrong, repugnant, by enhancing the beauty of the horses under her tutelage. Yes, she would take care of both of them. Her brain processed plans, short-circuiting from one thought to another as the black Ford Edge Crossover barreled down the highway to Florida.

Chapter 45

———

THERESA PUT THE MORNING coffee service on the dining room sideboard. Charles immediately poured a cup and then went out to the courtyard. The morning was a cool sixty degrees but the desert sun was warm on his face. He was surprised the police didn't arrest him after he confessed to shooting Victor, but he was put on their suspect list. They had told him not to leave town and that they would be scheduling a polygraph test. They told Charles they hoped Victor would regain consciousness so he could tell them what happened and if he saw the shooter.

Charles paced around the small garden, too restless to sit down. Henry joined him, slumped down on a patio chair, careful not to spill coffee on her heavy sweater.

"Any word from Rusty?" Henry asked her husband.

"No, no, nothing." Charles didn't look at his wife, pretending instead to pull a weed from the edge of a hydrangea plant.

The phone rang. Theresa called to them from the French doors leading from the dining room. She said the police were on the line. They asked to speak to Mr. Burns. Just as Charles took the cordless receiver from Theresa, Yuma slipped by Theresa and out through the French doors to join Henry with a cup of coffee. He sat in a chair across from her.

"Hello, Detective Williams? This is Charles Burns."

"Good morning, Mr. Burns. Have you heard from your daughter?"

"No, nothing."

"My team has been going through Miss Burns' and Mr. Bennett's computer. Miss Burns did not turn on her computer Friday, but the last thing Mr. Bennett did was to send an email to an Elizabeth Standish. Do you know who she is?"

"Never heard of a Standish."

"Yes, well, she evidently lives in Florida. Seems Mr. Bennett told her he would be in Florida next week and he was asking her to dinner, that he missed her."

Charles' face turned red, his knuckles squeezed the phone so tight he might have broken it in half with his vice-like grip. *That bastard,* he thought. *Cheating to the end. I hope he dies.*

"Mr. Burns, are you there?"

"Yes, I'm here." His voice turned threatening and both Henry and Yuma looked up at him. "The only person Rusty spoke of in Florida is a Stevens, in Ocala, and not too kindly. His horse won over a stallion Rusty was showing. Has there been any change in Victor's condition?"

"No. He's still unconscious. The doctor said it doesn't look good. Mr. Burns, my team will be out to your house. In fact, they should be there in the next few minutes. They're going to dust the bedroom again where Mr. Bennett was shot. I would also like your permission to search the house, and one other thing. An officer will be taking fingerprints of everybody who was on your ranch on the day of the shooting. Do we have your permission to do this?"

"Yes, but I don't know why you're going to all the trouble. I told you I shot—"

"Yes, we know you said you shot Mr. Bennett. Let me ask you about the gun you said you shot him with. It was wiped clean. Do you always wipe your gun off after you shoot it?"

"Yes. It's a peculiar habit of mine."

"Okay. As to the fingerprinting, it's just routine, something we have to do. Can you tell me who was on the ranch Friday?"

"Really, Detective."

"Just for the record, Mr. Burns."

"My wife and I, Victor and Rusty, of course, Yuma, and five or six ranch hands. I'd have to check with Yuma to see who they were and if they're here today."

Charles disconnected the call and laid the phone on the glass table in front of Henry and Yuma.

"What did the detective have to say?" Henry asked. "Is Victor conscious?"

"No. They found an email in his account, sent just before Rusty came home that day. The two-timing charlatan was making a date with an Elizabeth Standish in Florida."

Yuma staring at the phone on the table said "I heard Rusty accusing Victor of seeing a woman during the show. Victor didn't deny having dinner with her. He said she wanted to learn more about the Arabians, but Rusty wasn't buying it."

"Did the name Elizabeth Standish come up?"

"Yes, it did. Several times," Yuma said.

Chapter 46

———

THE POLICE OFFICER GRASPED Yuma's index finger, pressed it on the black ink pad, and then rolled it from side to side on the fingerprint card. He continued this routine until he had two complete sets of all ten fingers. After the last print, the officer handed Yuma a jug of hand cleaner and told him he could wash the ink off in the sink. Charles and Henry watched from the doorway. They and Theresa had already given their prints. Four ranch hands were waiting outside the back door for their turn.

Detective Williams sat at the kitchen table observing Yuma as his prints were taken. After he washed the ink off his fingers, the detective asked Yuma to come outside with him. He had some questions to ask him. They went out the back door and walked down the path to the barn.

"Yuma, is it fair to say you probably knew Rusty as well as anyone? Maybe even better than her folks?" The detective sat down on one of the hay bales leaning against a stall. Yuma sat on the other side looking back at Williams.

"I don't know about that, but I have looked after her since she was a baby … taught her how to ride. Of course, once up in the saddle we couldn't get her off that pony. Yes … even then she was strong willed, but she has always had a good heart. She cared for the animals, never one to use the whip. She'd whisper in their ears and they seemed to know what she wanted them to do. That's what made her such a good trainer. And grooming—she'd talk non-stop to the horse, and they'd whinny in reply. I swear they understood every word she said. But then—"

"But then, what?" Williams asked, quietly urging Yuma to continue.

The Indian looked off, out the other end of the barn and to the pasture beyond. "Well, sir, after she met Victor … she believed everything he told her. Her dream of being the best Arab ranch and his obsession with money seemed to bring the worst out of both of them."

"I saw the pictures you gave to the state's lawyer. Pretty damning evidence."

"It broke my heart to give them those pictures. But the horses … the operations … it just wasn't right. They felt pain for no good reason. They were beautiful to begin with. No need, no need to put them through it." Yuma wiped his eyes on his shirt sleeve. He took a handkerchief out of his pocket and blew his nose, trying to pull himself together.

"Do you have any idea where Rusty is?"

"Nope, except for one—she learned to fly. Has a pilot's license. She made me swear not to tell her folks. Wanted to surprise them someday. Take 'em to Vegas."

"I wished you'd told me this sooner. Where did she usually fly out of, Phoenix?"

"No, no. Too far away and too big. Glendale Municipal Airport is where she took lessons and she'd often rent a plane to check out an Arabian, mainly in Arizona, sometimes Texas. If you'll excuse me, sir, unless you have more questions, I have some chores to attend to."

"No, that's about it. Thanks, Yuma."

Yuma shuffled out of the back of the barn, pushed some hay to one side with the toe of his boot, and then threw himself up on Knight Rider's back. Detective Williams, watching Yuma ride slowly out of sight, yanked his cell phone off his belt and yelled at the officer who answered at the department.

"Check the Glendale Airport for a plane rental to Rusty Burns and sweep the airport's parking lot for her truck. If you pick up her trail, call me immediately. I'm heading to Glendale. If I'm not mistaken, I think we may have a lead on our elusive Miss Burns."

Chapter 47

———

BARBARA FOUND JERRY OUT in the barn, sitting on a bale of hay, leaning against Black Magic's stall. He looked up hearing her approach.

"You have a call, honey," Barbara said.

"Who is it?"

"He wouldn't say—just said he had to talk to Mr. Stevens, that it was urgent." Barbara handed her husband the phone and leaned against the stall door on the opposite side.

"Hello."

"Hello, Mr. Stevens?"

"Yes, Who's this?"

"My name is Yuma, we've never met, but I saw you at the Albuquerque show."

"Oh, I see, well if you're calling about a breeding, I'm not in the business anymore, I guess you could say I'm retired, but you can talk to the vets who store Black Magic's straws."

"No, sir, that's not why I'm calling."

"Then why are you calling?"

"To warn you."

"Warn me. Warn me about what?"

"I suppose you know Rusty Burns. She was showing an Arab stallion against yours at the show."

"Yes, I certainly will never forget Miss Burns. She wasn't too happy when her horse came in behind Black Magic."

"Well, I work for the Burns, have ever since Rusty was born. She's very high strung—"

"You certainly can say that about her."

"Well, we're afraid she's suffering a nervous breakdown. She was recently sued for fraud."

"I heard—word travels fast in our circle. I may be giving up the show ring but people in the business still keep in touch with me. I believe a Kuwaiti prince accused her of surgical alterations on a couple of horses he bought."

"That's right. She answered the charges, but when the judge didn't buy her reasoning it seemed to tip her over the edge. She lashed out at everyone around her, particularly her fiancé, Victor."

"I don't know a Victor," Jerry said.

"Victor is a veterinarian in the area or was until he gave up his practice. He moved in with Rusty and her folks and took care of her horses full time. Well, at that show, seems she caught him talking to another red head. Do you know an Elizabeth Standish?"

"No. An Elizabeth Stitchway lives here in Ocala. She was at the show."

"I don't know. Does she have red hair?"

"Yes, dark though—nothing like Burns'. Why?"

"Well, I doubt it's the same person. There was an email—definitely to a Standish. Anyway, Standish came to the barn area of the show. I talked with her a little. She was very interested in Rusty's horses. I don't know how they met, but I guess Victor and Standish had drinks and dinner that night, and he saw her again the next morning. All I can say about her is she was a talker ... asked all kinds of questions. She should have been a reporter."

"I don't know where you're going with this, Yuma."

"After Rusty appeared in court, it looked like she might have to pay a good percentage of the twenty-million dollars the prince sued her for, and maybe some jail time."

"To my way of thinking, altering a horse surgically, she should have been sued for more."

"I understand, Mr. Stevens. I didn't condone it either. But as I said, this sent her over the edge. Rusty and Victor had a terrible fight. Danged if she didn't pull out a pistol and shoot him."

"Good Lord, did she kill him?"

"No. The medics air-lifted him to a hospital in Phoenix. He's holding on by a thread. We don't know if he'll make it."

"I'm sorry to hear that, but I still don't know what that has to do with me."

"When she and Victor started fighting, she accused him of cheating on her with another red head—Standish. She also began ranting about Black Magic and his surly owner, which would be you."

"I've been called worse, Yuma."

"Maybe so, but not by a deranged woman. If she thinks she killed Victor, she may be headed to Florida to take out that other red head and that surly owner, if you know what I mean."

"Oh … I hear you. I'll talk to Liz about your call. Where is Miss Burns now?"

"That's just it. We haven't seen or heard from her since Friday—three days now. We don't know where she is … she's disappeared."

"You said you haven't seen her for three days. What kind of a car does she drive?"

"She has a red Ford truck, which we can't find either, but, sir, she's also a pilot. The police are checking the airports to see if they can find the truck, but no luck so far. Anyway, I just wanted you to keep on the lookout for her. We don't want anything bad to happen to her. She needs medical help. But in her frame of mind, believing she has already killed, well … you see what I'm afraid of."

"Yes, yes I do. Thanks for calling."

Jerry handed the phone back to Barbara. He stood up, brushed off his jeans, and taking hold of his wife's hand they began walking back to the house.

"Barbara, you know that electrician you talked to a while back?"

"About installing floodlights?"

"Yea, that guy. Call him and ask him to come out and go ahead with installing the floods. Use the specs we drew up."

"Okay, I'll call him this afternoon."

"Please, I want you to call him now. Tell him it's an emergency, but I want them installed by tomorrow afternoon. I'll pay him extra if he can get started today. Come on in the kitchen after you reach him and I'll explain."

Barbara stared at her husband as he headed for the kitchen.

LIZ FELT HER PHONE vibrate in her jacket, the display identifying the caller as Jerry Stevens.

"Hi, Jerry."

"Liz. I'm calling about a phone conversation I had about thirty minutes ago with a man who goes by the name of Yuma from Black Canyon City in Arizona. When you were at the Albuquerque show, did you meet someone by that name? He works for Rusty Burns."

"Yes, I remember him. Really nice man. I talked to him in the barn area. Rusty was showing a horse in the ring, so I took the opportunity to ask a few questions. Why?"

Jerry gave a half-hearted chuckle. "He remembers your questions—thinks you should be a reporter. Anyway, he called me about Rusty and Victor, whom I know you remember well."

"Whew, I sure do. Don't want to run into him again, but I did get the low-down on what he was doing to the horses."

"My guess is you won't be seeing him, at least for a while. He and Rusty had a fight and she shot him. He's in the hospital and they're not sure he'll survive."

"Oh, my God, that's awful. She really is a loose cannon isn't she."

"Yea, and that's why Yuma called me. Seems she's disappeared. Yuma thinks she's headed for a mental breakdown. She was sued by a guy she sold some horses to, some altered horses, and he found out about it. Sued her for twenty-million, and Yuma said it looked like she'd have to come up with most of it."

"What a turn of events in her life."

"Exactly. Yuma called to warn me and asked if I knew an Elizabeth Standish. I told him no, but I do know an Elizabeth Stitchway."

"Jerry, I sometimes use that alias when I don't want to divulge that I'm a PI. I gave Victor the Standish name. You said Yuma called to warn you. About what?"

"He believes Standish and I are on the top of Rusty's hate list. In that she's disappeared without a trace, she may be on her way to Florida. In her twisted way of thinking, Standish and I harmed her. Yuma said she accused Victor of two-timing her with Standish."

"Oh, oh. Maybe she saw him talking to me, or when he tried to, you know, kiss me in the parking lot when I was leaving for the airport. But, Jerry, if she's coming to Florida, she's still days away. The police should be able to track her down before she gets here."

"Could be, except she's a pilot. Yuma indicated she might rent a plane."

"Whoa, that changes things."

"Anyway, I wanted to let you know about his call. If you see or hear anything more, let me know, and I'll do the same."

"Will do, and, Jerry, thanks for the tip." Liz closed her cell and stood for a moment ruminating over what Jerry had told her. Then she returned to her desk and to the report she was typing on her laptop.

Chapter 48

———

RUSTY TURNED OFF INTERSTATE 75 at the Ocala exit and followed the signs to a Holiday Inn. She had made good time, arriving in Ocala just before noon, and had come up with an idea on how to flush out Elizabeth Standish.

After a quick shower and dressing in one of her new outfits, she fished around in her tote for the piece of paper with the telephone number she had written down the day before for Stevens' farm. Picking up the motel's phone, she dialed the number. A woman answered.

"Hello."

"Oh, hello. I wonder if you could help me. I was recently at a horse show in Albuquerque and met a very nice lady. I'd like to talk to her again but I lost her number. She mentioned she knew Jerry Stevens. Her name is Elizabeth Standish."

"You must mean Elizabeth Stitchway. She—"

"That explains it. Thank you."

Rusty hung up the phone. Smiling, she opened the telephone book on the nightstand. Thumbing through the new directory, she found two listings for Elizabeth Stitchway—one looked like a residence and the other a business with the page number for a yellow-page ad. Rusty flipped to the yellow pages and found the ad for Elizabeth Stitchway, Private Investigator.

"Well, well, a private investigator. How sweet. I suppose you were snooping around at the show gathering evidence against me. So that's why you cozied up to my fiancé. Bitch!" She tore the two pages out of the directory—the business ad and Stitchway's home address and phone number.

Rusty planned to pay a visit at night, but she surmised Stitchway would not be at her house on a Monday morning. Rusty thought it would be a good time for a reconnaissance trip.

Twisting her hair into a bun on the top of her head, anchoring it with clamps, she pulled the black-felt cowgirl hat she purchased in Baton Rouge down to her ears completely covering her flaming hair.

Leaving the motel she programmed her rental car's GPS system with two home addresses—Stitchway and Stevens. Following the GPS map, she navigated to the Stevens Arabian Horse Farm in less than thirty minutes. After turning off the highway, it was located off a narrow, paved road. There were a few houses, but mostly woods interspersed with pastures. This was horse country—pastures undulating over rolling hills. She reached the end of the paved road but there was room to turn around. There was also a dirt road off to her right.

Satisfied, she drove back on the main road and stopped to pick up a Starbuck's coffee and a turkey wrap at the sub shop next door. Following the GPS, she drove to the Stitchway address. Again she was on a rural road. Finding the number on the mailbox, she slowly passed the little cement-block house, with large spots of mold on the roof. Again satisfied with the results of her morning's excursions, she returned to her motel and waited for nightfall.

Chapter 49

———

NAVIGATING AROUND DRIVERS dashing back to their offices after lunch, Detective Williams pushed the button alerting him to an incoming call.

"Williams here. Watcha got for me?" He turned up the speaker on his phone as he sped down Black Canyon Highway to Glendale.

"Detective, Burns did rent a plane. She told the tower she was going to Las Vegas for a couple of days."

"Las Vegas?"

"They have no record of her landing on any airstrip in Nevada. So we sent out an APB on the plane's call numbers. We just heard from Baton Rouge. They have the plane. Landed early Saturday morning. The woman pilot said she'd be back in a couple of days and instructed the attendant to gas her up."

"And ... and what else—a rental car, motel, anything?"

"Sorry to say, that's it. She must be using cash. We finally got her bank to tell us if she made any withdrawals in the last few days. Get this, the day she shot Mr. Bennett, she must have gone straight to the bank and withdrew a hundred thousand."

"Well, that could hold her for a while."

"Oh, and one more thing. A Detective Milhous with the Ocala Police Department in Florida called us. Seems he knows a Jerry Stevens and an Elizabeth Stitchway, but not a Standish. I guess Yuma, that Indian, called Stevens warning him about Burns. Stevens called Milhous, yada yada."

"Okay, give me the detective's, number. I'll head back to the department. You go to the Glendale airport and question anybody who knows her and especially anybody who saw her when she rented the plane. See what else you can find out."

Williams cut the connection on the car phone. Seeing a rest area, he pulled off to grab a cup of coffee and to call Stevens. He also wanted to talk to the Stitchway woman, but she and Milhous could wait until he was back in the office. It was his guess that the trail had gone cold except for the fact that he was sure he knew where Rusty was headed. If only they could find her before something bad happened.

Coffee in hand, he called Stevens.

"Hello, Mr. Stevens? This is Detective Williams, Black Canyon City PD."

"Oh, hello. Hang on a minute. I have to turn over my eggplant rounds." Williams heard a scraping noise and then the bang of an oven door closing. "Okay. Did you find Rusty Burns?"

"No, but that's why I'm calling. Seems she rented a plane and landed yesterday, early in the morning at Baton Rouge. After that we have nothing. Mr. Stevens, I think she's heading in your direction. By the way, do you know an Elizabeth Standish?"

"You're the second person to ask us that today. Never heard of a Standish, but we know an Elizabeth Stitchway. She went to the Albuquerque show and met with Victor Bennett. I guess he made a pass at her."

"Bingo."

"Excuse me?" Jerry said.

"I think you have just confirmed, for me anyway, that Standish and Stitchway are one in the same. I understand you also know a Detective Milhous?"

"Yes, nice guy. I called him after receiving Yuma's warning," Jerry said.

"I guess he called me—does he also know Elizabeth Stitchway?" Williams asked.

"Yes. They both worked on a case for me. She's a private investigator."

Well, now isn't that interesting, Williams thought. "We think Burns is on her way to look you and Stitchway up. She's about a day ahead of us, which would put her in your area about now. I'll give you my cell number—if you see or hear from her, please let me know."

Jerry wrote down the detective's number and hung up. He immediately went into his office, opened the bottom drawer of his desk and pulled out his Smith & Wesson .357 revolver. He checked that the clip was loaded since the last time he and Tony went to the back pasture for some target practice. It was fully loaded. He placed the gun back in the desk's top drawer.

———

RETURNING TO THE KITCHEN, Jerry dialed Liz. She thanked him for the additional information and promised to keep in touch.

After Jerry's call, Liz and Maggie left the office and drove home. Liz entered her house and walked straight to her bedroom. Opening the bedside table, she picked up her Lady Smith & Wesson .38 Special pistol. The five chambers were loaded. She returned the gun to the drawer.

Chapter 50

———

LIZ paced from the kitchen to the bedroom, back again through the living room, Maggie following on her heels. She pulled a bottle of wine from the cabinet and then put it back. Maggie sat at her feet, tail brushing the floor.

"You're right. Let's go for a walk." Liz had already changed from her work costume into her red flannel jogging attire. She snapped the leash on Maggie's collar, flipped on the front porch light, and grabbed her jacket off the peg stuffing her cell phone in the pocket. The air was cool—the sun had set leaving a light-gray horizon.

After a couple of knee bends to loosen up, the woman and dog started to walk. Liz took a deep breath, filling her lungs with the cool, late afternoon air. Opening her cell phone, she called David. They were nearly to his house and she needed some moral support, or did she just want to see him?

David and Whiskey were already at the end of his driveway waiting for Liz when she and Maggie jogged up to them. Liz unclipped Maggie's leash and the dogs immediately took off into the woods.

"This is a nice surprise. Hope the girls don't corner another skunk." David took hold of her hand. "You seem a little preoccupied. Want a drink, glass of wine?"

"Oh, yes, that would be great."

They climbed the stairs as Whiskey gave a leap up to the deck followed by Maggie.

"Looks like Maggie's got the hang of bypassing the stairs," David said. "It's a bit chilly ... how about we go inside?"

"Can we sit in the kitchen? It's not so open as the living room."

"Happy day. Happy day."

"Sure. See, even Polly's happy to see you."

David watched Liz slide into the chair at the kitchen table as he poured her wine and a shot of Jack Daniels for himself. He handed her the wine and took a seat on the opposite side. She sat staring into her glass. David reached across the table and took her hand.

"Talk to me, Liz. You're not yourself."

"It's this Rusty thing."

"Yea. I talked to a Detective Williams in Black Canyon City. Did you give this Victor person your other email address, your Elizabeth Standish alias?"

"Yes. Victor sent me, rather sent Standish, an email last Friday saying he was coming to Florida and wanted to see me. I never replied. It was the same day he was shot."

"Well, I guess with Jerry's help, they now know you are Standish and that's why they think you are in Rusty Burns' cross hairs."

Liz took a sip of wine, then a deep breath, and looked up at David. "There, now I feel better. Thank you."

"Always like to be of service. Now, about this Burns woman. Can you get a picture of her?"

"Is your computer on … there's one on her website."

David led her to his den and sat down in front of his computer. Liz scooted him off the chair taking his place, her fingers immediately flying over the keyboard. Rusty Burns appeared on the screen.

"There's Rusty and down a little further … there, that's Victor."

"There's Rusty. There's Rusty."

"Thanks, Polly." Liz glanced at the parrot and then at the printer—it was on. She printed the page and handed it to David. Glancing down at the floor, she saw Maggie and Whiskey lying on the floor next to each other.

"Oh, David, I'm sorry. Maggie got your pillow. She has one at my office and at home. She kept taking one of mine off the bed so I gave her one."

"No problem, But I hope Whiskey doesn't get any ideas. Come on, let's go finish our drinks." They went back to the kitchen and

David refreshed her wine and another shot of Jack Daniels in his glass.

"Now," David said, again taking her hand across the table, "let's assume Rusty is on her way to Florida. And let's also assume she's coming to visit you and Jerry, and not in a friendly sort of way. Just to let you know, I've set up a cruiser to add your house and Jerry's farm to his route starting later tonight. How about you stay with me until we locate her? I have a spare bedroom."

"Thanks, but I'd rather be home. Besides you're doing a lot of assuming and don't forget Maggie's with me. Believe you me, she barks if she hears the slightest noise."

"Okay, but please keep your cell phone with you and promise me you'll call if you sense something's not right. Put on your PI hat—your instincts are good so use them."

"Will do," Liz said, trying to smile. "Maggie and I'd better get going."

———

LIZ PUT HER GLASS ON THE counter by the sink. Turning to say goodbye, David gently took her in his arms. He was going to say something but kissed her instead. Breaking his kiss sooner than he wanted to, he tilted his head back and looked into her wide eyes.

"I'm driving you home and no is not an option." David dug in his pocket for the car keys. They walked to the car without saying a word—the warm embrace filling his mind and easing its way into his heart. Opening the door to the back seat, both dogs jumped in. Liz had already settled into the front seat. Driving a short half mile, David pulled into her driveway.

"You know where I live?"

"Hey, you aren't the only detective in town you know." They got out of the car and David walked Liz to her door.

"Thanks, David."

"For what?"

"Letting me talk." Standing on her toes, she gave him a quick kiss on his cheek and turned to go in the house.

He waited for her to open the front door and then called out, "Be careful Stitch. Whiskey and I kinda like having you and your pillow snatcher around."

Chapter 51

—

WALKING IN A TRANCE to her kitchen, Liz could still feel David's embrace, his arms around her—so protective. It was a first for her. After being left by a fiancé in college, and the hint of romance with Rocket, neither involvement had felt like this. She gave Maggie a cup of dog food and grabbed a roll of string cheese from the refrigerator. Pulling the wrapper apart, she headed to the spare bedroom where she had set up her home office. Turning back, she snatched a box of crackers from the shelf and walked down the short hall to turn on her computer. It was only eight o'clock—plenty of time to do a little work.

Leaning back in the desk chair, waiting for the computer to finish the startup routine, she again felt the warmth of David's kiss. From the kitchen, she heard Maggie's low growl, then her nails clicking on the kitchen's white-tile floor to the window overlooking the backyard.

"I'm in here, Maggie girl."

Maggie didn't respond to her call. David forgotten, she immediately remembered Jerry's warning. Turning off the overhead light, she walked to her bedroom and retrieved her pistol from the bedside table. The kitchen light illuminated part of the hallway.

"Maggie, come here."

Maggie pranced down the hall and obediently sat in front of her mistress. She gave a soft bark, stood, and returned to the kitchen. Standing in the doorway, looking back at Liz, she growled again.

"Well, girl, something's bothering you, probably nothing, but we can't take a chance. The problem is that the only way to turn off that kitchen light is to go in there. The switch is around the corner, so if I ease down the hall, then swing around the corner I will be able to reach it."

Following her plan, Liz walked slowly down the hall, hugging the wall, gun held in front of her with both hands. Taking a deep breath, she swung around, her fingers touching the switch.

Bullets suddenly shattered the kitchen window. The kitchen plunged into darkness.

"Come on, Maggie. Let's get out of here." They darted out the front door, ran across the street and into the bushes. She stopped, stood still, listening, eyes riveted on her house searching for the shooter. All remained quiet. Nothing moved except the leaves overhead catching a gentle breeze. Liz took a breath, ran her hand over Maggie's silky head, and then darted again through the forest, running to David's house. She fought low-lying branches, tripped over stumps, but didn't stop. She could see David's driveway, the trees thinning out as she came to his property. Reaching the edge of the grass, she and Maggie paused, crouching low, deciding if it was safe to make a run for the deck.

Liz swore at herself, "Elizabeth, just call him for heaven's sake." Digging her cell out of her pocket, scanning the lighted display, she selected his number.

"Hello, are you calling for another pillow?"

"David, I'm outside, near your house," she whispered.

"What's wrong, Liz?" David, sensing she was scared, held the phone to his ear and at the same time walked out on to the deck. "I don't see you. Where are you?"

"Someone shot at me through my kitchen window."

"Are you hurt?"

"No, but I don't know who shot or where he is. Maggie and I ran out the front door … I don't know if we were followed … but I don't see anyone … there's no noise."

"Okay, hold on. Damn, a cruiser should have been watching. I'll call a couple of officers, at least one of them should be close by. Stay put … don't move."

"Don't worry, I won't." Liz pocketed her phone, knelt on the ground, her arm around Maggie.

Within minutes two police cars, sirens blaring came speeding down the road. One turned into David's driveway, the other came to a stop at the side of the road. The officers climbed out of their vehicles, each with a phone to his ear.

Whiskey reached Liz first followed by David. For the second time in one night, David enfolded her in his arms.

———

RUSTY, SEEING THE FIREPOWER, retraced her steps through the brush to her car. She had taken a chance and pulled into a driveway down the road. The house was dark so she presumed, hoped, no one was home. Without turning on her car lights, she backed out of the driveway and left the scene behind, driving away from the police cars.

Chapter 52

———

THE LIGHTS OF THE CRUISERS continued flashing red and blue, but the sirens were silent. David and Liz walked to the two officers now standing in his driveway.

"I think your sirens did the job—spooked her away," David said clearly irritated. "Where were you guys?"

"I drove by not more than twenty minutes before you called. You asked us to drive by—not a stakeout." The officer turned to Liz. "I'm sorry, ma'am."

"Liz, I don't think you should stay in your house tonight. How about taking me up on my offer of the spare bedroom?"

"No, I have another idea. That must have been Rusty. With the commotion from the squad cars I doubt she'll stick around. Like you said, I'm sure you scared her off, at least for now. I bet you she'll head for Jerry's farm."

"Okay, I buy that … so far. What's your plan, Stitch?"

"Let's give her a target she can't refuse … a two-fer."

"And that would be—"

"Jerry and I in the same place. I'll call him. Let him know that she shot at me."

"You think she shot at you," David corrected her.

"Yes, Detective, I think it was Rusty." Liz flashed him a smile. "In her crazy state of mind, she's not going to go home or wherever she's staying, and sit on the bed eating bonbons. Her adrenalin is flowing, ready to attack, and the sooner the better. Oh, one more thing."

"And that is?"

"You guys take me home so I can change and clean up these scratches," Liz said licking the blood off the back of her hand. "It'll only take me a few minutes."

"Okay. While you're cleaning up, I'll call Stevens to let him know he has company coming."

WHILE WAITING FOR LIZ TO change and bandage her hand, the officers came up with the logistics on how they were going to set a trap for Rusty. David would drive Liz in her car, leaving Whiskey and Maggie at his house. David would park behind the first barn concealing the car. The cruisers would park out of sight on the road picking the best vantage point to spot an approaching vehicle.

True to her word, Liz was ready in less than fifteen minutes. With assignments in place, David and Liz backed out of her driveway and began the drive to the Stevens' farm.

"You, okay? That was quite a scare you had. One of my guys swept up the glass from the window. He said to tell you to be careful in case he missed some." David gave her hand a squeeze.

"Thanks, I'm all right. What did Jerry say?"

"He thought it was a good idea that we come over. He's worried about Barbara's safety as well. And, he had another call from Detective Williams. Seems they picked up Rusty's trail as of yesterday. She stopped for gas outside of Gainesville and used her credit card to pay for it."

"Anything else?" Liz, her mind churning with possibilities of what they might face tonight, leaned her head back on the headrest.

"Victor died this afternoon. Never regained consciousness."

Liz sat up straight. "I didn't like him, but I didn't wish him dead either. From what we've been told, Rusty probably thinks she killed him in the first place, so one way or another, taking me out or Stevens—she's still going to be charged with murder."

Chapter 53

——

THE FOURSOME SAT SILENTLY in the Stevens' living room—Jerry and Barbara on the couch facing David and Liz across a coffee table in overstuffed chairs. The electric percolator on the sideboard provided the only sound, bubbling through the basket of ground coffee beans. Jerry, Liz, and David had each given a briefing of the events over the past two days. There was nothing more to be said. There was nothing more to do but wait. The only illumination in the house came from two table lamps in the living room and several under-the-counter spots in the kitchen.

The coffee finished perking—adding to the silence.

David spoke up. "Well, I for one could use a cup of that coffee." He stood, flexed his arms once, and walked over to the pot. Liz joined him.

Barbara fixed a cup for Jerry and herself.

It was almost eleven o'clock.

"How long do you think we should wait up tonight?" Barbara asked. "Just so you know, we have three spare bedrooms. I changed the sheets after you called, David. Wanted them to be fresh—you both are welcome to spend the night."

"Thanks," David and Liz said together.

Slapping his knees, Jerry said, "Well, I could use something to eat. How does an antipasto salad sound with piping hot sourdough bread?"

Jerry didn't wait for their answer. He was halfway to the kitchen before he finished his question. Barbara watched her husband disappear through the door, knowing he preferred to cook alone.

David pulled out his cell and called his officers on watch outside. They reported that nothing was going on. Not one car had driven down the road since they had arrived.

———

RUSTY DROVE IMMEDIATELY to the Stevens' farm. She didn't know it, but she had a twenty-five minute lead on Liz and David and his officers. She made her way from the utility road to the back pasture of the farm. She had seen the road just before the dead end on her reconnaissance trip. She figured the police might alert the Stevens' that she was in the area, on the other hand they could just as well be searching for her in Las Vegas. She saw the gate in the chain-link fence. A padlock dangled from the loop. It didn't look very strong to her. Looking around she saw a good-sized rock. She smashed the rock against the lock but it didn't give. She slammed the rock against it two more times and it gave way. She left the gate ajar knowing she would be returning for her car.

The Stevens' house was in the distance. It looked like at least one light was on from her vantage point. Jogging through the grass, she stumbled as a length of vine caught her boot, but she didn't go down. Her breathing became labored as she kept jogging toward the house. She was in an open pasture, so if anyone looked out that window they might see her in the moonlight.

She came to another fence, but this time it consisted of wooden rails. Looking in both directions she spotted the gate a few yards to her right. She knew she could have squeezed through the fencing, but decided to open the gate—again to facilitate her escape. She was now in the pasture. A gelding was grazing and looked up when she opened the gate.

In the pasture, there was only one more fence between where she was crouching and the lawn in the back of the house. She could now see that the light was on in the kitchen. A man was walking back and forth, pulling open cabinets and the closing them.

"You, bastard," she hissed. "Well, you won't be spreading any more lies about me. You and your high and mighty standards. Who are you to say what is morally right."

She quickly located the last gate between her and her quarry. Again leaving the gate open after she slipped through, she took her gun out of her jacket pocket and crept up to the bushes next to the house. Peering in the window she saw Stevens arranging food on a platter. He grabbed a mitt and opened the oven pulling out a loaf of bread. He put it on a wire rack and looked up. A woman entered the kitchen.

"Will you look at that, it's Stitchway!" Rusty whispered.

Quickly raising her gun, she pulled the trigger twice. Stevens fell from sight. Then Stitchway. Rusty turned and ran for the pasture. She knew if she tried to reach her car by running, surely someone would catch up to her. Seeing the gelding, she raced to him. Grabbing his mane she swung up on his back. Digging her heels into his side, the horse took off.

"Come on, boy, you can go faster than this," she yelled. "Hi Hi, come on. Go. Go." Rusty kept yelling, speeding through the gates—only one more ahead.

———

HEARING THE GUNSHOTS, David and Barbara ran to the kitchen. Jerry and Liz were on their feet. Jerry yanked his shirt off over his head and looked at his arm. A small amount of blood was trickling down to his elbow, dripping to the floor. Liz quickly wrapped the wound in the white dishtowel hanging out of his pocket.

David, cell phone to his ear, yelled, "You guys see anything? She just shot out the kitchen window. Nothing? I'm telling you she's out there?"

"The utility road—Barbara, show David the utility road." Jerry cried out.

Liz knotted the towel and Jerry ran for the back door. "I'll take the tractor. Meet you at the south pasture."

David yelled again in his phone, "You guys know about the utility road? Down back ... yes, south end of the property ... I don't know where she is."

With his cell to his ear, David ran after Liz and Barbara who were nearing the barn and her car. He punched another code on his phone.

"David, the key. Toss me the key." Liz shouted.

"Hey, Bob, send two more units to the Stevens' farm." He tossed the key to Liz as he climbed in the front seat beside her. Barbara slammed the back door and Liz gunned the car following Barbara's instructions as she yelled when to turn.

"I want you to surround the house, expand out in a grid, flush her out of hiding." David closed his phone and clung to the roll-bar handle as Liz yanked the steering wheel to the right. The car now tore down the dirt utility road.

"There's a bend up ahead," Barbara yelled, hanging onto the back of Liz's seat.

They heard the tractor off to their right, catching its headlights bobbing over the ground as it continued to speed to the south pasture.

———

HEARING A SIREN IN THE distance, Rusty streaked through the chain-link gate. On she went, clinging to the horse's mane, knees clamped to his side, up on the ridge, down to the road.

Suddenly lights hit the gelding in the face, frightened he reared up, hoofs in the air crying out in alarm, throwing Rusty in the air. Screaming she landed on her back, rolled to the side. Pulling her gun from her waistband she shot wildly at the headlights in front of her. Suddenly headlights pierced the darkness in back of her. Wincing in pain she managed to turn and shoot at the approaching car, but her gun was empty. She threw the gun to the side and began to wail. "I got you Stitchway. I got you."

David, Liz, and Barbara climbed out of the car and ran to the woman writhing in the dirt. Rolling in pain, knees to her chest, she continued wailing, sobbing, screaming at the officers as they approached.

"Get away from me. Get away from me," she screamed, sobs racking her body. The officers quickly approached her and cuffed her ankles, fearing a back injury they left her wrists free.

An EMT van came bumping down the dirt road, skirted Rusty's rental car, dodged Liz's car and stopped. Hauling a stretcher from the van along with a board to brace her body, the EMTs and two other officers carefully lifted the screaming woman, curled up in a ball, onto the stretcher and into the van. With just enough room to turn the van in the opposite direction, the driver slowly made his way past the vehicles and then disappeared from sight at the bend in the narrow road.

———

DAVID ASKED ONE OF THE officers to bag the gun Rusty had thrown on the dirt. Barbara checked the towel on Jerry's arm peeking underneath to see the wound.

"You're lucky, hon. A few inches to the right and she would have hit your heart," Barbara said tucking the ends of the towel under.

"I'll wash it off when we get back to the house," Jerry said. "Can you lead our horse back to the upper pasture. I think she broke the padlock on the new gate. I didn't stop to look when I jumped off the tractor. I'll pick you up in a few minutes." Jerry turned to David, "I guess that wraps up the excitement for tonight, Detective. What will happen to her?"

"The EMTs are taking her to the hospital. They'll give her something to calm her down and make a determination if she has to spend the night there or can be transferred to the jail. I'll call Detective Williams to let him know we have her, and we'll start the process to remand her to his custody. He'll probably fly here tomorrow to pick her up, providing she's physically able to make the trip."

"Thanks for your help, David, Liz." Jerry nodded to each of them and then trotted back to his tractor.

David looked at Liz, concern in his eyes. "You, okay?"

"Yes. But I'm glad it's over." Liz stood, arms hanging limp by her side.

"How about you and I go rescue our dogs from Polly and share a nightcap?"

"Sounds wonderful, although I hope we find you still have a bird when we get back. Our dogs are both hunters, so she may be missing a few feathers."

Chapter 54

———

RUSTY LEANED DOWN TO massage her leg where the ankle bracelet was digging into her skin. Detective Williams had accompanied her from Orlando International Airport to Phoenix. A judge ordered a thirty-day stay, under police guard, in a hospital for observation of her mental status. A Black Canyon City officer was driving the detective and Miss Burns to the hospital but first they were making a stop at the Burns' ranch.

The detective had a few loose ends in his case and he was hoping that with Rusty in the house where the shooting occurred he might have an opportunity to tie up those loose ends.

"We'll be at your ranch for maybe an hour," the detective said, turning to Rusty sitting beside him in the backseat of the car.

Rusty didn't reply. Leaning back, she stared out the window at the barren desert as the black and white police car sped up Black Canyon Highway.

Henry greeted her daughter, scooping her up in her arms the minute she stepped out of the car. "Thank God, you're home safe."

Rusty didn't hug her mother, nor did she fight to move out of Henry's embrace. Feeling no response, her mother stepped back allowing Rusty and Detective Williams to walk through the front door into the large foyer. Henry and Charles hesitated, not sure what to do, but Rusty continued walking into the living room and straight to the mini-bar. She poured a shot of whiskey over some ice cubes and then sat on the couch, curling her legs underneath her. Facing the large fireplace built of desert-colored flagstones reaching up through the cathedral ceiling, she stared at the electric picture frame, the present on her twenty-first birthday. The picture on display was of Rusty at twelve years old.

Charles and Henry followed their daughter into the living room. Charles also visited the bar and Henry took a seat in a wingback chair to the side of the couch.

"Would you like a drink, Henry? I think I'll join Rusty."

"Yes, that would be nice. Detective, would you care for a drink, or maybe a cup of coffee?"

"No, thank you for asking."

Charles handed Henry her drink and then sat down in a matching chair facing Rusty.

Rusty took a sip of the whiskey, closing her eyes to savor the bitter taste. Opening her eyes and staring again at the picture on the stone mantel over the fireplace, she said in a monotone, "Why did you say you shot Victor, Dad?"

Charles leaned forward, his arms resting on his legs, head down, remained silent.

"Detective Williams said Victor died a few days ago." Rusty took another sip of her drink.

"Yes, that's right, dear," Henry said.

The doorbell rang. Theresa passed by the living room, saw the family, and quickly turned away. She greeted another officer and led him through the foyer into the living room.

"Please have a seat, officers," Charles said, drawing up two small chairs completing the circle.

Detective Williams introduced Officer Simmons to the Burns family and then the two officers sat down.

"I asked to meet with the three of you to discuss Mr. Bennett," Detective Williams said. "As I explained, Mr. Burns, I'm escorting your daughter to a hospital for observation. She has also been ordered to wear the ankle bracelet at all times."

"Yes, we understand," Charles said glancing at Rusty and back to Williams.

"Miss Burns you are being charged with the death of Mr. Bennett, and the attempted murder of Miss Elizabeth Stitchway and Mr. Jerry Stevens as I informed you when I picked you up in Florida. I also read you your rights at that time. We have a couple of problems with the Bennett case. As I also told you yesterday, your father confessed to shooting Mr. Bennett and relinquished the gun lying on his desk. Forensics examined the weapon and the bullets matched those that were shot at Mr. Bennett—they were fired from that gun. But then the facts of the case become blurred."

Detective Williams stood up, walked to the fireplace, looked at the picture of a young Rusty Burns riding a pony. The ticking of the grandfather clock standing in the corner of the room provided the only sound.

"You see," Williams said turning back to the group, "The gun had been wiped clean except for one set of prints."

"I told you I killed him," Charles said. He returned to the bar and refreshed his drink, this time without ice.

"Well, whoever pulled the trigger on that gun, whether it was Miss Burns, or you, Mr. Burns, wiped the fingerprints off her gun, a gun registered to her, but miraculously none of her fingerprints were found, leaving one fresh set of yours, Mr. Burns. The bullets certainly contributed to Mr. Bennett's death, but the two shots fired from that gun did not kill Mr. Bennett."

"What are you saying, Detective?" Henry asked leaning forward in her chair, her eyes locked on Williams.

"The autopsy showed that Mr. Bennett suffered a fatal stabbing to his chest with what appeared to be a blade of a hunting knife."

"That's preposterous. Rusty ran out of the house after a fight with Victor. She and I were the last to see him. I shot Victor and the 9-1-1 call was made. You and the medics arrived—no one else entered the room." Charles scoffed at the idea and downed his drink.

The room fell silent, the clock pendulum swung back and forth—breaking the silence at the hour of two.

Rusty looked up at the detective. "Yuma has a hunting knife. He carves wooden horses with it."

"Thank you, Miss Burns. Officer Simmons, please stay with the family. I'll pick up the other detective outside and take a ride to the barn to talk with Yuma."

"He's probably at his house. He has lunch about this time." Charles said. "I'm coming with you."

Ten minutes later, not finding Yuma in the barn, Detective Williams rapped on Yuma's front door, opened it, and stepped inside. Yuma sat at a pine kitchen table facing the open living room and the front door.

He looked up at the two officers and Charles now standing in front of him. On the table lay a leather sheath next to a hunting knife, the blade reflecting the sunlight streaming in the window.

"I was waiting for you, Detective. I'm sorry, Mr. Burns."

Rusty and Officer Simmons quietly entered the room—the three men at the kitchen table were unaware of their presence.

"But, Yuma, you weren't there." Charles leaned on the table looking into the eyes of his long-time and trusted friend.

"I was coming to see Rusty and heard the two of them fighting, Rusty and Victor. When I heard the shot … Rusty was running down the hall and never saw me … I rushed in the room and saw Victor lying on the floor crying. He looked up at me, pain in his eyes, asking me to help him. I only saw the pain he had inflicted on all those horses, my blood turned to fire, I had to stop him. Never again would he cut a horse." Yuma picked up the knife and put it in the sheath. "I ran out the way I came in through the back entrance from Rusty's wing leading to the barn. I rode Knight Rider up to the plateau above the ranch. Falling to my knees, I cried out to God, to please forgive me for what I had done."

"Yuma, no," Rusty screamed. She ran to the old Indian, knelt beside him, threw her arms around his waist, and laid her head in his lap. Clinging to him, sobbing. "Yuma, what have I done to you. How blind I was not to see how much I was hurting you, hurting everyone. Yuma, please, please forgive me."

Yuma looked down at the distraught woman and saw the little girl with red curls who had brought him such joy.

"There, there, Rusty. You just got all mixed up in your head— followed Victor instead of your own moral compass. You lost your way."

"Yuma, what do I do?' Rusty was sobbing uncontrollably as she continued to wrap herself around her mentor and best friend.

"You must respect the law as I must." He continued to cradle the little girl, stroking her fiery hair. "You must listen to the doctors. They will help you find your way back."

She looked up at Yuma with her tear-stained face. "But, Yuma, I need you, I need your help. Yuma … no, no, it's my turn to help you. Yuma, I promise—I'll help you."

Rusty continued to look at Yuma's lined face, into his eyes, into his soul. Her body straightened, strengthened. Grasping his leathery hands, she pulled him to his feet. "Someday you and I will ride to the plateau … ride together again … I promise."

Epilogue

———

CHRISTMAS CAME AND WENT at the Stevens' farm. Jerry cooked up a storm trying to dispel his depression over losing Black Magic. The only decoration in the house was a large spruce tree in the foyer set ablaze with a myriad of tiny white lights. While the decorations were sparse, the house was filled with the aromas of the season emanating from the kitchen—cookies and pies as well vegetable casseroles topped with cheese, butter and breadcrumbs. But there were no guests.

It was almost midnight on New Year's Eve, and Jerry was still in the kitchen. Carrots, onions, and potato cubes jumped in the bowl of the food processor as Jerry pulsated the button. Satisfied, he dumped the contents into a large mixing bowl. Cracking an egg into the mixture and emptying a bag of tofu, sausage-flavored crumbles on top, he began stirring the mixture with his hands.

Bursting into the kitchen, Barbara beamed with excitement. "Jerry, did you hear the phone ring?"

"I did, what's up?"

"Desiree's water broke. Linda's on her way. Come on, let's go."

"You go ahead. I'll be down as soon as I clean up the kitchen."

Barbara's shoulders slumped. "Okay, but you're going to miss the birth. He's Black Magic's son you know."

"Of course, I know. I'll be down soon."

Barbara left the kitchen filled with disappointment. She had hoped the new foal would bring Jerry out of his depression. Quickening her stride to the barn, her disappointment eased and she began to smile. Smiling at the thought of the new foal, her spirits brightened. *Maybe there's still a chance. Please give us a little miracle,* she prayed.

Linda was already in the stall watching Desiree's progress when Barbara quietly slipped in beside her. Desiree, lying on the fresh straw, head up looking back, waiting for her foal, gave a soft whinny.

"Good girl." Barbara kneeling beside the mare stroked her neck. "How's she doing, Linda. Everything look okay?"

"Yup, here he comes."

Barbara looked at her watch. It was just past midnight.

In slow bursts, the foal's little hoofs could be seen in the sac, then his head. The sac split apart, a hoof protruding. Linda pulled the sac back a little revealing his head. Within minutes the baby was clear of his mother. He inched close enough to Desiree so she could reach him, licking away the membrane that had cradled him in her womb for so many months.

"Linda, he's beautiful."

"He sure is. All his vitals are strong," she said, putting her instruments to the side.

Both women looked up sensing Jerry's presence. He stood silently looking over the stall door at the fuzzy baby.

The foal tried to stand, but he didn't make it. Desiree, careful not to step on her baby, stood up, the cord connecting to the foal broke away. Linda immediately dipped it in disinfectant.

Jerry stepped quietly into the stall. He put his arms around the newborn and helped him to his feet, holding him to be sure he was able to stand, then slowly took his hands away.

"He is a beauty ... isn't he." Jerry looked up at his wife as a tear cascaded down his cheek, a smile slowly spreading across his face.

Barbara looked through her tears at her husband. "Yes, honey, he's going to be a winner."

The colt, standing on wobbly legs, turned his head nuzzling Jerry's sleeve.

"His coloring. Barbara, have you ever seen a deeper bay, a richer bay? And his mane and tail are Black Magic through and through—black as ink."

"Jerry, look, look at that fluffy tail—it's flagging, I swear."

"Hey, look at that pose," Linda chimed in. "It's show time."

"Do you think?" Jerry asked looking at Linda.

"Yes, I think. Once he grows out of that baby fuzz, he looks to me like a true Arabian."

The foal stood by his mother and then laid down on the hay to rest.

"Well, I think I'll be going," Linda said, picking up her bag. "Looks like everything is under control here. I'll be back later this afternoon to check on him."

"Thanks, Linda, I'll walk out with you." Barbara gave Jerry a quick hug, a peck on his check. "Happy new year, honey." She left him caressing the baby's neck and whispering to the foal—the newest member of the farm ... the *little* miracle.

The End

REVIEW REQUEST

Dear reader, I hope you enjoyed meeting a new friend, Elizabeth Stitchway. If you have the time, it would mean a lot to me if you wrote a review, your honest appraisal. What did you like most? It's super easy. Go to Amazon. Log in. Search: Mary Jane Forbes The Mailbox.

Thank you!

ADD ME TO YOUR MAILING LIST

Please shoot me an email to be added to my mailing list for future book launches: MaryJane@MaryJaneForbes.com

The Author

BLACK MAGIC is Mary Jane Forbes' sixth novel. Thinking she would take a month or two off, a new inspiration came her way and she is off and running doing research for a new project. She says the dust bunnies will have to stay under the bed a little while longer.

Stay tuned at:

www.MaryJaneForbes.com

Black Magic, An Arabian

ISBN: 978-0615949390 (sc)
Printed in the United States of America
Todd Book Publications: 012/1/2010
Second Release: 09/2017
Port Orange, Florida

Author photo: Ami Ringeisen
Cover photograph: Arabian horse by Trolev, Dreamstime.com
Cover re-design: Mary Jane Forbes

Acknowledgements

A big thanks to Shannon Luznar, who gave me my first glimpse into the new age of horse breeding with artificial insemination. I first saw a story in my local newspaper featuring Dr. Luznar's business—Equine Reproduction Center of Central Florida. She graciously agreed to an interview where I met her husband, Mike Kondracki, co-founder of the business, and Ashlie Turner, Office Manager. The rest, as they say, is Black Magic.

Thanks to Roger and Pat Grady for their scrutiny of the first draft. Once again, their efforts made for a much cleaner story.

As ever, thanks to Vera and Adele for giving me initial feedback and catching some of those pesky typing errors.

… and, to my daughter, Molly. It never ceases to amaze me how she comes up with salient, constructive criticism while tending to a husband and five children.

Thanks to my brother-in-law, Dick Colton, who did some initial sleuthing in Arizona for me. I once lived near Black Canyon Highway, Route 17 from Phoenix up to Flagstaff. His mission was to find me a city off this highway. Hence, Black Canyon City is where the western part of the story resides.

Thanks to Tim Cicchella, Ocala Development Corporation of Marion County, Inc, for information about Ocala.

Dear reader, as you settle back in your comfortable chair, I hope you enjoy meeting some new friends and catching up with Elizabeth Stitchway in her business as a Private Investigator.

Books by Mary Jane Forbes
Fiction

Bradley Farm Series
Bradley Farm, Sadie, Finn
Jeli, Marshall, Georgie

The Baker Girl
One Summer, Promises

Twists of Fate Series
The Fisherman, a love story
The Witness, living a lie
Twists of Fate, daring to dream

Murder by Design, Series:
Murder by Design
Labeled in Seattle
Choices, And the Courage to Risk

Elizabeth Stitchway, PI, Series
The Mailbox, Black Magic,
The Painter, Twister

House of Beads Mystery Series
Murder in the House of Beads
Intercept, Checkmate
Identity Theft

Novels
The Baby Quilt ... a mystery!
The Message...Call Me!

Short Stories
Once Upon a Christmas Eve, a Romantic Fairy Tale
The Christmas Angel and the Magic Holiday Tree

Visit: www.MaryJaneForbes.com